The Price of Love

Book #2 in the Rockin' Country Series

By Laramie Briscoe

Edited by: Lindsay Gray Hopper
Cover Art by: Kari Ayasha, Cover to Cover Designs
Proofread by: Dawn Bourgeois
Formatting: Paul Salvette, BB ebooks
Photography by: MHPhotography & Custom Stock Photos
Cover Models: Jack & Ashley Edmund

Dedication

Love & marriage is not always easy. It takes work, compromise, and a whole lot of forgiveness. Luckily for me, I have a husband who excels in all of those things and more. He's one of the reasons I do this. If it wasn't for him, I probably never would have pursued it. Thank you, Michael! You're my kinda bad boy, but you've definitely got the tattoos and piercings!

Summary

Wife
Husband
Superstar entertainers
Two people completely in love

Harmony and Reaper thought life would be easier once they sealed the deal. Stage personas put to the side, settling into marriage should have allowed them to be Hannah and Garrett to the world at large.

Boy, were they ever wrong!

Pressure from record companies, fans, and the people surrounding them put their brand-new union under the strain of the entertainment machine. Long nights apart, quick meetings in hotel rooms, and new faces on the music scene were not what either of them thought they would have to contend with.

When love is strong, emotions go haywire, and frustration is at an all-time high, everyone's true colors are revealed.

Hannah and Garrett have a decision to make—is fame worth the price of love?

Chapter One

Two weeks. Two long weeks. That was how long it had been since Hannah had seen Garrett in person. Sitting downtown at her favorite restaurant on McGavock with her mom, she was trying desperately to stay involved in the conversation they were having, but it was becoming harder and harder to keep her mind from wandering.

"Hannah," Elizabeth Stewart snapped her fingers. "Are you even paying attention to me?"

"Sorry, Mom, I zoned out there for a minute," she apologized, looking down at her barely eaten sushi. What was normally her favorite meal when she was home just didn't hold the appeal that it usually did. "I didn't sleep very well last night."

"Miss your husband?"

Hannah's face burned hot. How did she tell her mom that memories of the two of them together kept her up at night? Those little snippets of conversation here and there along with nightly talks over Skype and FaceTime weren't getting the job done anymore. She needed to feel his arms around her, needed to feel his lips against hers, really wanted to smell the spice of his cologne. She missed it all.

"Yeah, I do," she sighed, twirling her wedding ring on her finger with her thumb. Recording had amped up for both of them, and this was the longest stretch they had been apart.

"Well I guess it's a good thing he just got here, huh?" Her mom shrugged nonchalantly as she took a sip from her wine glass.

"What?" Hannah understood the words that were spoken, but her brain couldn't comprehend them. Garrett was thousands of miles away on the opposite coast. There was no way he was walking into a restaurant in Nashville.

"Look behind you." Liz pointed behind Hannah's shoulder.

Still unsure of what was going on, Hannah turned around in her seat and a squeal ripped free from her mouth as she saw Garrett making his way into the restaurant. Not even caring who saw, she launched herself into his arms, squeezing him tightly around the waist. She felt her feet leave the ground as he tightened his arms around her and bent his knees to pick her up.

"You're really here?" she questioned in his ear, almost like she didn't believe he would have made a special trip for her. She ran her hands through his hair, over the slight beard that covered his face. She even caressed the earrings in his ears, delighting as she felt the coolness of the metal. It was another reminder that this wasn't a dream—he was here with her, holding her in his arms.

He pulled back so that he could look her in the eyes.

"I'm really here."

"How?"

"Why don't we go sit with your mom?" He gently pushed her towards the table her mom sat at.

"Nice to finally see you again in person, Garrett. I thought that from now on all of our conversations would be conducted over a cell phone line," Liz laughed as she stood up and gave him a hug.

"Me too."

"Wait? The two of you have been talking to one another?" Hannah asked as she sat back in her chair, her mouth hanging open in surprise.

"You could say that." Liz smiled, a conspiratory look in her eyes.

Garrett's arm went around her shoulder as he sat closer to her, pulling her as close to his side as he could with the arms of two chairs separating them. "I thought she was lying about you missing me, because when I talked to you, you seem fine, but then I realized how sad I was and figured you were just as sad. So I flew out to see you. I missed the hell outta you."

"But how did you even get his number?" Hannah questioned. She was very careful with all of his information. The last thing either one of them needed was for people who shouldn't to get hold of their private conversations.

"Shell may have had something to do with it." Liz winked.

Shell was another person who missed someone terribly. "Please tell me that Jared came with you to see her." Like her and Garrett, Shell and Jared Skyped, texted, and FaceTimed, but it wasn't the same as seeing a loved one in person.

"He was on his way to check into a hotel for the night. Something about them having 'time to themselves'." He used air quotes with his fingers, a mischievous smile on his face. He knew exactly what Jared wanted to do with their time to themselves.

Hannah played with her chopsticks. "She tells me how much she loves him every single time I talk to her about him. I'm glad he came to see her."

"Do you want to order something?" A waiter asked Garrett as he came over to the table.

"Are we gonna be here long enough? I'm about to starve." His belly picked that moment to growl loudly.

The ladies laughed and Hannah put her hand on his. "I think we'll stick around for you."

"You know what I like, order me something." He indicated for her to speak to the waiter.

"With whatever she orders, I'll take whatever beer you have on tap."

Hannah quickly ordered, and the waiter promised to have it out as soon as possible.

"So what have you two ladies been doing today?" he asked as he looked between the two of them, situating himself so that he had Hannah next to him, his arm lazily slung over the back of her chair.

"We're having lunch and then we're shopping."

"You don't have to do that now," Liz protested.

"No, Mom, I want to! Garrett can come with us." She grinned as she bumped his side.

"I'm sure he doesn't want to do that."

"I have a sister," he deadpanned. "I do lots that I don't want to do, but I daresay it would be a pleasure to go with the two of you."

Hannah pursed her lips and looked at her mom, shaking her head. "He's a charmer and he can't even help it. I can see that you're falling for it too." She shook her finger in her mom's direction.

"He is very good," Liz laughed. "I can see now why you were missing him and why you married him."

"What do you think of this?" Hannah asked Garrett as he stood in the middle of one of her favorite boutiques. She held up in front of her a sundress that was a bright yellow color.

Glancing around, he noticed that Liz was on the other side of the store. He approached Hannah with a smile lifting up the corners of his mouth.

"What?" she asked, tilting her head to the side.

He reached in and traced where the vee of the neck would lie on her chest, running his finger along the exposed skin there. "Looks like it might be a little low-cut."

"Oh yeah, I'll wear a tank top underneath it." She licked her lips, looking down at his finger.

Leaning in so that his mouth was even with her ear, he said, "You wouldn't have to do that with me. You wouldn't even have to wear *unmentionables* with it."

The smooth, dark tone of his voice caused her to close her eyes and lean heavily against him, her knees no longer able to hold up her weight. She turned her face into his neck and nipped him there with her sharp teeth. "I missed you," she whispered.

"Missed you too," he answered her back, running his hand through her hair. "More than you fucking know." He moved away from her when he saw Liz approaching and cleared his throat. Didn't matter if he had put a ring on it, he still felt weird showing the kind of chemistry they had in front of their parents. "So you're gonna get that one?"

"Yeah. Mom, what do you think?"

"I love the color; the yellow will go well with your darker hair. It's a little low-cut though. I think you're gonna need to wear a camisole or something underneath it."

Hannah hid her smile. "I was planning on it."

Liz's phone went off, and she struggled through her bag to find it and answer it. "It's your dad, I better take this."

They watched as she walked off for some privacy.

"I really hope that he's calling her and asking her to come home. I love her, but I haven't seen you in weeks," she blurted out, causing Garrett to laugh.

He put his hands in his back pockets and rocked back on his heels. "We'll be alone soon enough. It was really nice of her to set this up for you. I don't think you would have been honest with me about how much you missed me."

"There was nothing that we could do about it. Record companies are record companies."

"True, but we could have asked for a few days off." He put his hands on her shoulders and rubbed there. "I've been dreaming about you for the last week. I feel like I'm not sleeping at all."

"Funny that you should mention that. I've been

having some pretty...vivid...dreams myself."

His dimples appeared in his cheeks, and he ran a hand down her arm before clasping their fingers together. "I can't wait to hear this."

"I don't know that you'll *ever* hear it." Her face flamed. "But know I had them, okay."

He opened his mouth, but quickly shut it as Liz made her way back over to them. "I need to go. Your dad needs help at the shop."

"Okay, Mom, I had a good time today." Hannah hugged her tightly. "If you wanna get together tomorrow, just let me know."

"I'll talk to your dad and see what he wants to do," Liz commented, holding her arms open for Garrett.

"It was a pleasure seeing you again after spending so much time talking on the phone." He gifted her with a smile.

Hannah noticed her mom's cheeks getting red. She couldn't help but shake her head. Even her mother wasn't immune to Garrett's charms. They watched Liz walk away, and Hannah pinched his side. "You are way too cute for your own good," she laughed.

"What can I say? Women want me."

Chapter Two

Hannah gripped Garrett's hand as they walked down West End towards his car. She loved being in Nashville, even though it wasn't exactly easy for the two of them. Here, they didn't have to worry about paparazzi, and people weren't surprised to see them walking down the street. They could be more free here.

"I'm so excited you're here," she said again, gripping his arm with her free one. She clasped his left hand and gingerly ran her finger over his wedding ring. It still gave her a secret thrill that he was the type of man who liked to wear it and didn't take it off.

He swung her bag in the opposite hand and smiled down at her. "I'm excited to be here too. It only sucks that I'm not here for longer."

"How long did you get off?" she asked as the two of them approached the car.

Garrett walked her to her side and opened the door for her, playing the gentleman for her, before walking over to the driver's side and having a seat behind the wheel. "I flew in today; I'm here all day tomorrow, and my flight leaves at eight p.m. the next day."

Not long enough at all, but they would do what they had to do and enjoy the time that they could get together. She bit her lip to keep her emotions at bay. The two of them had chosen this life and they had chosen to get married—no one had forced them to do either of those two things, but sometimes being responsible really sucked.

"I guess Shell already left," Hannah laughed, seeing a note on the kitchen counter. She leaned down, reading the hastily scribbled handwriting, as she put her bags atop the granite.

"Is it weird for you that she still lives with you?" Garrett asked, throwing the car keys next to the bags and having a seat on one of the bar stools that made up the kitchen area.

"Why would it be weird?" She shook her head. "Do you not want her living with me?"

This was a slippery slope, Garrett realized, but he'd already opened his mouth. "When I come here, I kinda just want to spend time with you; we get so little of it."

She could see where he was coming from, but she couldn't kick Shell out; she'd lived here ever since Hannah had bought the little craftsman bungalow. "I don't know what the solution to this problem is." She laughed nervously.

He got up from where he sat and walked around the counter. "Maybe it's time for me to put roots down here too. I think it's time for us to take the step of finding something together."

This was big, huge in her mind. Even though the two of them had been married for almost four months, they'd never bought anything together. Purchasing a home together signified something she had been scared to hope for from him. Ridiculous, she knew, but a slow smile covered her face.

"What?" he asked, smiling back at her.

Hannah walked over to where he stood and slipped her arms around his neck. "Buying a house is something that married couples do!"

He chuckled, one dimple showing in his cheek. "Well, babe, we are married." He held his left hand up to show the wedding ring she'd put on there.

"I know, but we don't get to do too many of the things that normal married people get to do."

Garrett smiled slowly. "Then we'll do this, and we'll devote ourselves to it while we're recording. I want to do every imaginable *married* thing possible."

That warmed her heart; it always did when he said things like that. There was a part of her that worried he would get sick of her, that he hadn't honestly been ready to settle down and be with one woman for the rest of his life. Every time he said things like that, it chipped away at one more little piece of resistance.

"I love you," she told him, reaching up and capturing his lips with hers.

"I love you too," he mumbled against her lips.

Garrett buried his hands in her hair, sighing when he tilted her head to his liking, finally able to capture her lips the way he wanted to. It had been a couple of hard weeks in the studio. He and the guys were being rough on each other, and he had a ton of tension he needed to release. Before Hannah that had meant going out to their favorite bar, drinking themselves into oblivion, and finding some random chick to go home with. Now, he didn't have that but he needed it. He needed his wife like he'd never ever needed her.

Grasping her hips, he lifted her into his arms, taking a moment to thank God that she'd worn a dress. He pulled his lips back from hers, burying his face in her neck and inhaling deeply. He had missed her scent terribly. That scent let him know that she was with him and she wasn't going anywhere. Running his hands along her thighs, he clasped them around her back and walked them over to the counter. Once he sat her there, he pulled back, his green eyes connecting with hers. He loved when she looked like this, her eyes hazy, her lips swollen, and her cheeks red, because he'd done that for her, to her.

"I missed you so damn much," he whispered before grasping the back of her neck in his hand and melding their mouths together again.

Hannah wondered what had happened in the weeks since they had seen each other, usually their time together like this wasn't so intense. He wasn't as finessed as he normally was, he was taking her the way he needed her. She wanted to question him, but it was obvious that he didn't want to talk.

Running his hands up her smooth legs, Garrett separated her thighs, making room for his body in-between them. With rough movements, he unbuckled his belt, pushing his pants down just far enough so that he had room to work. His long fingers grasped her hips and pulled her to the edge of the counter, pulling her panties aside. "Sorry, but I need you," his voice was guttural as he pushed into her.

The truth of the matter was, she needed him too, any way he needed her. Hannah loved to be whatever he needed her to be, that's what she had always dreamed of when she thought of marriage. Digging her nails into his shoulders, she hung on for dear life as he took her hard. She moaned when his arms came around her back, holding her in place for him, to keep her from sliding.

Garrett buried his head into the crook of her neck, nipping the slope of her shoulder with his teeth. He brought one hand back up to her neck, digging his fingers into her hair and tilting her head back to expose her neck to his mouth.

"Damn, Han," he groaned as he used his teeth to nip at the strong column of her throat. When she sighed the sexiest sigh he'd ever heard from her mouth, his release hit him like a punch in the gut. He couldn't stop it any more than he could stop the earth from spinning, the sun from shining, or from loving this woman that he held in his arms.

Hannah was right on board with him, thrusting her hips against his, leaning up so that she could bury her face in his neck. She had thought this would end—the feelings that she got whenever they were together, the almost painful way her heart constricted when he held her like she was the most precious thing in the world to him.

He felt the rush of her breath there and sighed, clasping his arms more tightly around her. "I fuckin' missed the hell out of you," he breathed, willing his heart rate to slow down.

"I got that." She grinned, pulling back and gazing up at him. "Are you sure nothing else is wrong?" It wasn't the fact that he had taken her quickly, or even hard; they had done all of that before. This time, there had been a desperation in his movements, like he was scared of not holding her close enough, scared that she would leave.

Garrett had to look away from her probing eyes. He pulled out of her body and hitched his jeans back around his hips, before turning away from her.

"What's wrong?" she asked, trying to hop down from the counter, but her legs were too short and she struggled before finally making the leap. It wasn't graceful, and she was grateful that his back was turned to her.

How did he explain to her, when he wasn't sure himself? "I feel stifled."

"By me?" she whispered, her heart stopping. Surely to goodness after what they had shared, he wasn't going to ask for a divorce. Right?

"No, no, no." He held his hands out in front of him as he turned back around. "I want to make a record that's completely different from anything we've ever done before. The rest of the guys are with me, but the record company isn't. Our producer is even liking the stuff we've brought to the table, but they don't want to budge. They don't want to give us that freedom."

The politics of having a record deal. Now that she could understand. "What are you gonna do?"

"I don't know," he sighed.

She could tell it was weighing heavily on him. The one thing, as an artist, that you didn't want to do was compromise, but at the same time, your family still had to be fed. "Have you thought of making the album you want to make and then giving it to them? Letting it stand on its own merit? You guys are big enough that you aren't going to have an exec with you in the studio, over your shoulder, every day. Finish the album, hand it to them, and then be like, 'peace out'."

A smile spread across his face and he laughed. "Peace out?"

"Yeah," she giggled right along with him. "Peace out. Let's face it, the fans that love Black Friday are probably going to gripe that it's not the same music that you've put out before, and they'll complain for weeks about it, then that song will hit number one, and the album will release at number one. The record company will then wonder why they ever doubted you. Just keep what you're doing under your hat until you're done. Use some of your old demos that they haven't heard before."

"Goddamn, you're a genius sometimes." He reached over, kissing her on the cheek.

She shrugged, her eyes avoiding his. "I may have done it once or twice myself. Sometimes, as an artist, you just know. It may be the worst mistake you've ever made in your life, but Garrett, your fans are so rabid…they're gonna love anything you do."

This, right here, was exactly what he had been missing. Someone who believed in him no matter what he wanted to do, no matter how bad of a decision it might be. He needed her confidence in him. There were only so many times he and the guys could try to pump each other up—at some point, it had to come from an outside source. At that moment, he yawned loudly, his jaw cracking from the force of it.

"You tired?" she asked, reaching her hand up to cup his stubbled cheek.

"Yeah, I've been worried, so I haven't been sleeping."

Grabbing his hand, she led him through the house, to her double-headed shower, turning it on before he even had a chance to speak. "Let's get cleaned up and go to bed."

"At," he checked his watch, "six o'clock?"

"We're on our own time here." She waved him off. "Besides, it's been way too long since I got to sleep in your arms."

"Tomorrow, maybe we can talk more about getting a house?"

She grinned. "Yeah, we can talk more about you buying me a house."

The light-hearted joke did more for him than anything could have, and he knew without a shadow of a doubt that working in some days off was exactly what he had needed. He vowed he would make the most of it— time with her was precious and he wasn't going to waste it.

Chapter Three

Garrett opened his eyes and took in his surroundings. The sounds were different than those in his Huntington Beach home, and he could feel warmth beside him. He knew that was Hannah, and knowing that made him happier than he had been in weeks. It wasn't the same without her; no matter where he was, he wanted her with him. There was a part of him that wasn't full unless she was beside him. He felt like half of a person without her, and that scared him, but he knew that was part of giving his heart to someone else.

Rolling over, he opened his arms to her and snuggled her against him. She came willingly and gave a soft sigh of contentment as he ran his hands up and down her back. He slowly reached over, not wanting to wake her, and grabbed his cell phone. It was 5:30 a.m.; they had slept for almost twelve hours, but now he wanted to do something with her. They had few precious hours left. Clearing the sleep from his throat, he put his head next to hers and whispered.

"Babe, wake up."

She stirred beside him, burying deeper into his body.

"It's too early," she protested.

"But we slept for twelve hours. I don't wanna waste any time with you. Let's go do something."

She sat up, huffing the whole way.

"You're so cute," he taunted.

"Seriously? If you're going to get me up this early, I'm going to need a coffee."

He laughed, grabbing her around the waist and pulling her to him. "What can we do?"

"Go get coffee." Her eyebrows were raised, her tone smart.

"We'll do that, but what else can we do at 5:30 in the morning. Is there a place we can go walk or something?"

Every other time he had been to Nashville, it had only been for a day at a time, and it made sense that he wanted to do something besides lie in bed with her. That didn't mean that she wanted to do lie in bed all day either, but any other activity this early in the morning was bordering on divorce territory.

"Fine," she sighed. "We can go run or walk at the park. Is that good for you?"

"Perfect." He smiled brightly.

"I am going to murder you one morning, I swear," she grumbled as she got out of the bed and walked over to her dresser.

He watched her, his gaze unabashedly running the length of her body.

"Stop ogling me and get ready." She threw the shirt she'd slept in at him, covering his face with it as he laughed.

"You embarrass me," she heaved as they ran in Centennial Park.

"Is it my tattoos?" he asked, as he looked at his bare arms in the tank top that he wore.

"No, not you embarrass me, you are embarrassing me because I'm huffing like a smoker and you're not even winded." She stopped for a second, putting her hand deep into her side.

"It's because I have to work out a lot when you aren't around. Working out wears me out enough so that I can go to sleep without you there," he admitted to her, walking circles around her as she massaged the stitch out of her side.

She rolled her eyes, but the smile on her face was unmistakably tender. "Sometimes you're too sweet for your own good," she told him.

"Hey, just doing my job." He held up his left hand, showing the ring that he wore. "Besides, aren't you glad I work out for you?"

Hannah stopped heaving a moment to take in the picture that he made standing there before her. The tank top he wore was soaked with sweat from the late-summer Nashville heat, even this early in the morning; the black hat he wore backwards on his head was wet around his forehead, but little rivulets of sweat made their way down his face and to the strong column of his throat. His skin was red with exertion, but that caused his tattoos to stand out in stark relief, and her eyes immediately searched out his newest one, a musical note on his left bicep that intertwined with a script H. That was hers and hers only. His black athletic shorts hung low on his hips, causing her to lick her lips. She was pretty sure she looked like she'd just run a marathon while he looked lickable.

"Don't get me wrong, I am. I only wish I look as hot as you do working out," she grumbled.

"If you could only see what I see." He caught her around the waist and spun them around in a circle, causing her to squeal.

It was so different here; he realized it each time he came to Nashville. There were people who saw them together and asked for a picture or autograph, sometimes they took pictures of the two of them, but those people never invaded their space. They didn't have to be quiet so that others wouldn't know that they were there. They could be just like any other newlywed couple. He was thankful that she was able to give them this experience. He knew they wouldn't be able to have it in California. There were too many people there that made their money off invading others' privacy.

She opened her mouth to say something, but he gripped her hips, his fingers tickling her sides. "Stop," she laughed, trying to get away from him.

"Well if it isn't the hottest married couple in the world right now," a voice said behind them.

Garrett didn't know who the man was that ran in place behind them, but he was interested as to why he felt the need to come up and talk to them.

Hannah laughed, smiling as she turned around. "Hey, Bryson." She reached over, giving him a friendly hug.

Bryson. Garrett had heard that name more than a few places. This was one of the new hotshot country rockers that liked to wear tattoos and piercings just like he did. He'd actually listened to a few of the other man's songs and he liked them, but he did not like the way Bryson watched his wife.

"Garrett, please meet Bryson Grant, the next big thing in outlaw country."

Garrett put his arm protectively around Hannah, pulling her closer to him before offering his hand. "What's up? I'm Garrett."

"Nice to meet you." He pumped Garrett's hand enthusiastically. "I'm a huge Black Friday fan. It's an honor, man."

"Thanks, I've heard a few of your songs, I like what you have going on."

Hannah looked between the two of the, not liking the way Garrett's body stiffened and the way he gripped her harder against him.

"Well, it was really good to see you, Bryson." She smiled at her friend. "But we need to go get some breakfast, I'm starving."

"See ya around, Hannah." He waved as he jogged in the opposite direction.

She eyed Garrett closely. "There is no reason in this world for you to be jealous. He and I are friends that go way back. I mean, we went to high school together. That's how far back it goes," she told her husband, putting her arms around his waist.

His mind told him that she was right, there was no reason for him to be jealous; she loved him, there was no doubt in his mind that she loved him. It ticked him off that he couldn't be with her all the time when there were a million other men that could.

"High school, huh?" he asked as they made their way to the car.

"Yes, he saw me in all my awkwardness. There is no way he would ever have any inkling of a reason to want me," she laughed.

"Now that's a fuckin' lie." Garrett shook his head. "You're hot, regardless of what you think."

She screwed her mouth up at his language. "C'mon, feed me, I'm hungry." She grabbed his hand and dragged him back to their car.

Garrett cranked up the AC when they got back to the car as the two of them sat, cooling off and gulping down water. "You are hot, ya know?" he told her, turning so that they could face one another.

"So are you, but that doesn't mean I can get jealous of every girl that takes a picture with you or knows your real name. Once I do that, I give them power." She pointed to a group of people that had cameras trained on them.

"At least they're not real paparazzi," he told her as he reached over and cupped her chin in his hand. Their lips met in a kiss that meant everything in the world to both of them.

No one would be able to break the bond they had unless they gave someone else power. It would be something that they would have to constantly remind themselves, they both knew it and at the same time knew they couldn't forget it.

Chapter Four

"I don't care. I hate the idea," Hannah argued with Shell as they sat in the recording studio, going over new songs for the day's recording session.

Garrett had left the day before, and Hannah had been in a foul mood since. They'd managed to look at a few houses together, but even thinking back to that experience wasn't making her happy.

Shell shook her head. "Bryson is the hottest thing going right now besides you. It would do you both good to record a duet together."

"The only duet I want to record is going to be with my husband, please understand that. I wrote this song for him, I can't sing this with someone else." Hannah hitched her chin up at a stubborn angle.

"Well, you learned the fucking chin hitch from him, I'll give you that." Shell blew out a frustrated breath. "Do you want to be labeled as someone difficult to work with?"

"No," Hannah cried. "What I want is to for everyone else to take my marriage as seriously as I take it," she yelled before getting up and slamming out of the studio.

She quickly walked to the exit and out into the night. She had a seat on the curb and looked down at her cell phone. She calculated the time difference in California and hit a button on her pre-sets.

"Hey, babe." His voice was smooth and deep as it came over the phone.

"Hey." She sniffed, not even sure why she was crying. She was so mad.

"What's wrong?" he asked.

In the background, she could hear him up and moving. She figured he was going somewhere they could have a private conversation.

"I'm really angry," she told him, her voice trembling.

"Who pissed you off, sweetheart? I'll murder them if you want me to." It always scared him how true that statement was. He didn't want anyone to ever hurt her, and when someone did, it physically made him angry.

She laughed, but it was watery. "Jared might be mad at you."

"Shell?"

"Yes, and I hate being mad at her, but she's asking me to do something that I really don't want to."

This was the part that Garrett hated. He wanted to be there for her, he wanted to hold her in his arms when she had hard decisions like this. He wanted to be the person she came to, to talk it through. But here he was, three thousand miles away on the other end of a telephone. "Why don't you tell me what happened? I'm sure it's not that bad and the two of you are just being bitchy with one another."

She wished that was it, but she had a feeling as soon as she told him what Shell was asking her to do, he'd be just as mad. "They want me to sing a duet with Bryson," she cried softly.

He inhaled sharply, seeing red. "As in the dude I met the other day that you went to high school with?"

"Yeah," she whispered.

He shifted in his seat, already feeling anger course through his body. Someone came in the room and he barely heard them.

"Garrett, we need you."

He turned, snapping at the poor intern that had been sent to get him. "You can damn well fucking wait until I'm done talking to my wife."

She sighed. "There's no reason to bite someone's head off," she scolded him softly.

"Now I'm pissed. What kind of duet?" He had to know. If it was what he was thinking, he'd hop the next plane himself. He wasn't sure what he thought he was going to do, but he was one thousand percent behind his wife on this.

It wouldn't do the either of them any good if she lied to him. "It's a love song, the song I wrote for you."

"Oh fuck no, hell-to-the-fuck no, not in this lifetime, babe, will you be singing a love song with anyone but me. Is Shell out of her fucking mind?"

"I think so." She held her head in her hands. Times like these, she was so tired. All she wanted was to be a normal wife to her husband, even if he was Reaper of Black Friday. These were the times when she thought that maybe she should give her career up. She'd never voiced those thoughts to anyone before, and she wondered if now was a good time for that. "Please say something," she pleaded.

"I'm amazed that Shell would think this is a good idea," he barked at her.

"There's no reason for you to yell at me, Reaper." She used his stage name on purpose. He was ticked, she was ticked, neither of them needed to yell at anyone. It wasn't a good time, but she knew that this was probably going to be the first real screaming match they'd had with each other. Words and feelings were too close to the surface.

"I'm pissed." He held his hand out to his side, even though she couldn't see him. "You would be too."

She was, which was why she was on the phone, listening to him rant, while she really needed someone to calm her down. "What do you want me to do?" she asked, running a hand through her dark hair. "You tell me what you want me to do and I'll do it."

"Whatever the fuck you want to do," he growled into the phone.

"Are you kidding me?" she yelled into the receiver. "I called you, upset because of what they were asking me to do. I didn't want to do it, I called you so that you could make me feel better! Right now, you're making me feel like I'm cheating on you. Do you think I want to do this?"

"I think what you want is to make me make the decision for you. I think that maybe you still aren't strong enough to stand up for yourself." His tone was soft, but the accusation was there.

"I can't believe you just said that to me," she hissed.

"Sometimes the truth hurts." His tone was smartass and it even made him recoil.

"You know what? I don't want to talk to you anymore." She hung up, feeling vindicated when she heard the dial tone before he could even say goodbye.

How dare he? She had called him because she hadn't wanted to do what they were asking of her, because she needed his support, and he'd been a jerk to her. He had always told her that sometimes he wasn't a nice guy, but he usually was with her, and she did not like the jerk that he could be. She put her head in her hands and let a few tears squeeze through her eyelashes. It felt good to cry and not have anybody see.

"Hannah, are you okay?"

She groaned when she heard the voice of the person who was causing the issue at hand. "Hey, Bryson." She sniffed, wiped her eyes, and attempted to smile up at him.

"Are you okay?" he asked again as he had a seat next to her.

Hannah couldn't help but gaze at him since he sat right next to her. His left arm displayed a sleeve of tattoos, and he wore a skull ring on his left ring finger. He had a goatee on his face and a black hat, backwards on his head. If he were taller, leaner, cockier, he would be Garrett's younger brother.

"No," she breathed heavily. "I'm not."

"Is there anything I can do to help?" he asked.

She pushed her hair behind her ear; he grabbed her left hand as she brought it down.

"Your engagement ring is different," he laughed, running the tip of his finger over the black diamond.

The way he did it felt weird. She didn't like it when anyone other than Garrett touched her ring. Pulling her hand away from him, she sat it down on the curb. "Yeah,

Garrett doesn't do normal very often." She smiled sadly.

"What's got you so upset?" he asked.

She glanced over, his dark eyes told her that he wanted to know, that he was worried about her. Since he seemed to be the only one who gave one iota about her right now, she sighed. "Please don't take this the wrong way, but I don't want to do this duet with you."

Bryson frowned. "It's just a song, Hannah."

"No, it's not." She jerked away from him and stood up. "It's not just a song. When I sing, I put everything in me into that song. I absolutely cannot sing a song about love with anyone but my husband."

"It's like acting." Bryson grinned.

The boyish look on his face told her that he didn't get it. He didn't have anybody to love and he'd never truly been in love. If he had, he would know why this made her so mad, why it seemed to spit in the face of her marriage. "I'm not an actress," she retorted. Now he was beginning to make her as mad as everyone else was. "When I sing, I put a piece of myself into it. I can't fake loving someone besides my husband, and I won't sing with anyone but him about love, especially this song. I don't know what you and everyone else can't understand about that. This is my decision and I'm deciding not to do it."

The phone that she held in her hand began ringing, and she bit her lip as she saw Garrett's picture there. "I have to take this."

Bryson looked like he wanted to say something else to her, but she waved him off, answering the phone call.

"I can't believe you hung up on me." Garrett's voice on the other end of the phone was full of frustration.

"I can't believe you were being such a jerk to me!"

He sighed and she could imagine him sitting somewhere, his long legs stretched out in front of him, or maybe he had his elbows on his knees. She hated this.

"This is hard," she whispered.

The whisper broke his heart. "It's a lot harder than I thought it would be." The laugh he managed was hollow.

"I think seeing you made it worse," she admitted.

"I think you might be right about that, but right now I need to see you. Go to the car and FaceTime me. We need to talk."

She answered with a simple yes and hung up. Quickly, she texted Shell, letting her know that she needed some time, but she would be back when she was done. Walking over to her car, she unlocked the doors and had a seat in the driver's seat. If she closed her eyes and inhaled deeply, she could still smell Garrett. It didn't make things any easier, but it at least gave her some comfort. She pressed the button that would connect them by video. When he accepted, she couldn't help but smiling at his face. No matter how mad she was at him, he could always brighten up her day.

"Hey," she said softly, biting her bottom lip, feeling almost shy with him.

He blew out a frustrated breath. Her face was red as well as her eyes. It was obvious that she'd been crying, and he hated that. "I don't want to argue with you."

"I don't want to argue with you either. I mean, I called you to talk some sense into me and you flew off the handle."

His look was sheepish. "I know. I'm embarrassed that I did that, but I don't like it. It seriously makes me very angry that Shell's the one asking you to do it too. She knows how I feel about you. She knows how you feel about me."

"I'm angry with her too, but she's only doing what the record company asked her to do. Bryson was here, he said if I sang with him it would just be like me acting."

Garrett saw red. He did not like this guy one bit. "And what did you say?" It was a supreme effort for him to hold his voice, his attitude, in check, but he did it for her.

"That I'm not an actress."

He laughed, one side of his mouth hitching up in a grin. "I love you," he laughed again.

"I love you too, and that's why I can't do this. They're just gonna have to get over it."

The two of them were quiet for a few moments until she spoke again, this time not meeting his eyes through the phone. "You know, sometimes I wonder what it would be like to only be your wife."

"What do you mean?" he asked, his eyebrows screwing together in question.

"Not being Harmony Stewart, only being Hannah Thompson."

His face was soft as he gently talked to her. "That's not what you want and we both know it."

"I don't know," she answered. "Sometimes I do want it."

Chapter Five

"Have you calmed down enough to see reason?" Shell asked as Hannah made her way back into the studio.

Hannah fixed her with an icy glare, putting her hand on her hip. She was tired of this, tired of trying to defend herself, and now it looked like she had to defend her marriage too. "I have. I talked to my husband and he supports my decision."

"He would."

The words were said under Shell's breath, and they made Hannah mad all over again. Deciding she was done for the day, she grabbed her stuff and started packing it into her bag.

"Where are you going?" Shell asked, confused.

Hannah sighed. "I'm done for the day, so I'm going home. Nobody cares what I have to say about anything anyway. It's not like you need me here for anything."

"We still have two hours left," Shell told her, checking her watch.

"No, we don't. I'm going home."

The sound guys, Shell, and Bryson, who had come

into the studio, were all speechless as she finished packing her stuff and walked out the door. Nobody tried to stop her as she made her way to her car and got in. Once there, she sat in the driver's seat, breathing deeply. Starting up the car, she drove around to nowhere in particular. She needed to clear her head and shopping would do just that. As she was making her way to one of her favorite boutiques, the dashboard screen lit up, telling her that her sister-in-law, Stacey, was calling.

"Hey," she answered, happy to talk to someone who wasn't a part of the issue-at-hand she was dealing with.

"Garrett called me, pissed at the world. I'd like to hear your side of the story. Figured you'd like to talk about it."

Garrett and Stacey were close, and in the months since he and Hannah had gotten married, more and more, he went to Stacey to try to see Hannah's side if they argued. They tried hard not to take things out on each other and to wait until they had both calmed down so that they could talk things through rationally.

"They want me to record a love song with another artist as a duet," she sighed. "I don't want to do it, but Shell's pressuring me, which means the record company is pressuring her. Garrett's mad, I'm mad, the other recording artist thinks it's funny, and Shell's about had enough of me."

"I can't believe that Shell, of all people, would ask you to do that," Stacey mused across the phone line.

"I know! That's why I'm so angry. She knows what my marriage means to me, she knows how badly I miss Garrett, and she knows *me* better than almost anyone in this world. I know she wants what's best for me, but sometimes I could give a care less if I sell another million albums. At this point in my life, I just don't care," she whispered.

"Is it not what you want anymore?" Stacey asked, her voice soft.

Tears clouded Hannah's vision, making her pull over on the side of the road. "I'm not sure what I want right now. I know that I don't want to make a snap decision, but everybody keeps pushing me in that direction."

"No, you're more sure than you think; otherwise, this wouldn't be so hard for you."

Hannah gripped the steering wheel then slammed her fist against it in agitation. "I'm almost twenty-five years old, I'm a newlywed, and I'm in love for the first time in my life with someone who loves me back. Not the me he sees on stage either, the real me. I want to bask in that, glory in it. Our honeymoon was three days long, and we haven't spent more than that together since we got married."

"You want a break?" Stacey could hear the frustration from Hannah, and to a point, she could understand it. She felt this way with Brad sometimes—the band and his career would always come first. Their lives would always be expected to come second.

"I do," her voice was strong. "I've never really taken one. It's always been a few weeks here, a few weeks there, maybe a month. I've gone from tour to record and back three times since I turned eighteen. I've not had more than a month off in almost seven years. I need a break."

"What will Shell say about that?"

"I'm not sure, but going to rehab for an eating disorder was the only freakin' long-term vacation I've had. That's sad."

Stacey had to agree with her. Someone with her star power, who had sold millions of records, should be able to get a vacation. "You need to have your lawyer read through your contract; there should be some clause in there that says you get time off. Garrett and the guys have taken a year off at three different points that I know of."

Hannah bit her lip as she rolled that over in her head. What would the record company say if she did find the clause and she exerted her power? She was like any other human being in the world. She was feeling tired and used up; she'd been feeling it more and more lately. Another part of her wondered if they would let her do it. She had one more song to record, and then the record would be done. A boatload of money had already been spent on this, and she had a feeling they wouldn't let her walk away from it.

"Thanks, Stace, you've given me a lot to think about."

"Sometimes it takes someone who's not in the situation to see it clearly."

Truer words had never been spoken. A lot of the time, she and Garrett had such strong feelings about who was right and who was wrong, they argued over the stupidest of things. Wanting to deflect that attention, Hannah pulled into the parking lot of the boutique, grateful that this was the day of the week they were open late. "How did Garrett sound?"

"He was pissed at first—you know that his temper starts out hot. Then, as we talked more, he sounded sad.

He misses you."

"I miss him too. We could have picked a better time to get married. Our lives are so crazy."

Stacey laughed. "The first day I met you, I knew that Garrett would marry you. You ground him in a way nobody else can, but at the same time, you're a trigger for him. All it takes is someone saying one thing about you that he doesn't like and he flies off the handle or comes to the wrong conclusion. It hurt him a lot that they want you to do a love song with someone who's more your type."

"Is that what he said?" Hannah was shocked those words had come out of his mouth. "Someone more my type? I've never heard anything more ridiculous in my life. There is nobody in this world more my type than him. I didn't know it when I first met him, but now, without a shadow of a doubt, I know it."

"You make him insecure in a lot of areas I've never heard him be insecure about before. When you aren't with him, his mind wanders." Stacey knew that she shouldn't be telling her sister-in-law these things, but Hannah needed to know. She needed to know that it wasn't one-sided—the fear that this could all go away tomorrow. It was very much felt on both sides.

Garrett's insecurities were completely stupid, and Hannah knew she was going to have to have a talk with him. There was no reason in this world for him to believe that he needed to be insecure over them. "Okay, I'll talk to him. I'm gonna let you go," she told her sister-in-law.

"Alright, if you need anything else, give me a call!"

"Love you," Hannah told her. "Thank you for listening to me."

"Love you too. Come visit soon!"

They hung up, leaving Hannah to stew. She knew exactly what she needed to do and she knew exactly who she needed to contact. It was time to go over Shell's head. With a sigh, she dialed the number for her lawyer.

"What the hell, Hannah?"

Shell came storming into the house that the two of them shared, waving a paper around, later in the afternoon.

Hannah had been mentally preparing for this since she'd gone to her lawyer's office. "Exerting some of the clauses in my contract and my authority."

"There was a time when we would have talked about this," Shell fumed from where she stood.

"I tried to talk to you about it, but you shot me down. The only duet I'm going to be singing is going to be with my husband. It's up to the record company now, if they want to ask his record company. If you read the whole thing, you saw that I'm touring for eight weeks and that's it. I'm taking a year and a half off after that. I deserve it, and it was in my contract to be able to do that."

"What about me, Han? What am I going to do for a year and a half? Have you thought about that?" Shell hated to call her out on it, but this felt too selfish to her. Her whole life was tied up in Hannah and her business. Now, because Hannah was married, she was going to forget one of the people who had helped her get there?

Hannah had given some thought to that. "You're gonna still be paid. Be a girlfriend to your boyfriend, spend some time with him, and find a hobby. Be normal. We haven't done that in so long, Shell. I want it so much. I need it so much."

The fight went out of Shell and she collapsed on the couch. "This is really what you want?"

"It is, and I want you to be happy for me. I want you to do all the things that you've never been able to because we've been on the road. I want you and Jared to have what Garrett and I have."

The two of them were quiet for a long time.

"It scares me, you know?" Shell admitted.

"What does?"

"Spending all that time with Jared and not having you to do things for. What if I get on his nerves? What if you decide that you don't need me anymore? What if you never come back to this, then where is my life and what do I do about all the time I've put into it. The love you have for Garrett is amazing and beautiful, but it worries me that you're going to give everything up for him. I know I'm being selfish, but I can't help but think of it. I've spent most of my adult life making sure you have everything you need and that you're okay. You don't need me anymore."

"That's not true at all." Hannah put her arms around Shell's neck and hugged her tightly. "I'm going to always need you, but I need him too. Life changes, it evolves. If you give Jared the chance to be your Garrett, he could be."

"I know," she grinned. "Maybe that's what scares me the most."

"It's time for us to stand on our own. We've depended on each other for a long time, and now, we've got to do it apart."

"I know." Shell wrinkled her nose.

"When Garrett and I find a house here, this one is yours. I know you love it here, and I would never take your home away from you. Maybe you and Jared can make some amazing memories here."

That sounded good to Shell. At least she wouldn't be in this alone, she did have Jared, but she worried that she wouldn't ever be enough for him. It would only take one thing to set him back, and she worried she was a trigger for him more than a help at times. Although she would never admit that out loud.

"Thank you." Shell hugged Hannah back. "You know, as mad as I was at you earlier, I was proud too, 'cause you stood up for yourself."

"I've got to. If I don't, people are going to walk all over me and they are going to ruin the only things that make me happy in life. There's more to life than when the next record is coming out and which tour we're going to do next."

That was a very mature way to put things, and again, Shell was impressed. "What do you think Bryson's going to say?"

"I don't really care," Hannah laughed. "He and I have been friends for a long time. If he's still my friend, then he's going to understand."

Shell laughed along with her, but there was a small part of her that wondered if Hannah knew exactly what she was doing. This could be the end of Harmony Stewart if they didn't play this correctly, but this was Hannah's decision to make and Shell knew that she would have to support her, no matter what.

Chapter Six

"That's it, Hannah," the sound engineer in the booth told her. "We're done."

"With the whole thing?" she asked, holding her headphones to her ears tightly, afraid that she might have heard him wrong. She knew they were getting close, but she hadn't realized they were that close.

"With the whole thing! Go enjoy yourself for a week or so while we mix this and get record company approval."

"You'll send me the finished copy of everything?" she questioned.

He nodded, giving her a thumbs-up as she took the headphones off her head and made her way out of the booth.

"I think you've got somethin' special here, Hannah," he told her. "You're voice has gotten much more mature, and you seem more comfortable with yourself. You're fans are growing up, just like you are. They're going to appreciate the changes that you've made in your life, and they're going to be able to tell that you're comfortable in your own skin."

"I am." She smiled. "I love the changes that I've made in my life."

He reached up, giving her a hug. She had worked with Brett since she'd started in the business. He'd been the sound engineer on every single one of her albums. "They look good on ya, doll."

She hurried around the studio, grabbing up her stuff. "When should I have the final product, do you think?"

He glanced at his watch. "Today's Wednesday. I'd say by Friday of next week. Go have yourself a mini-vacation. Go visit that husband of yours."

That was exactly what she was thinking too. "Thanks for workin' so hard, Brett." She reached down, giving him a hug around the shoulders.

"I only work as hard as the artist, and you, my friend, work your ass off. You deserve this break that I've heard rumblings about."

She bit her lip, shifting her weight from one foot to the other. "Do you think I'm makin' a mistake? You've been doin' this a long time."

"If you were a flash in the pan, I would tell you to strike while the iron is hot and don't you dare take any time off. That you need to capitalize on everything you've got. But you're Harmony Stewart, and you've changed the way we do things here on a certain level. You write amazing songs, you're sweet, but at the same time you're learning not to take any shit off other people. I say if you want to take some time off, you'll be fine. If you're burnt out and pissed off at the world, you're not going to do anybody any good."

"I need this time off," she re-iterated. "But then I look at the long line of female country singers that took time off, that never made it back. LeeAnn Rimes, Shania Twain, Faith Hill. They're still very respected and big names in the industry, but they never made it back."

"They were also older than you when they took a break," he raised his eyebrows. "And their breaks were years long. Not to mention, they didn't have hot rocker husbands, like you."

She smiled, a blush covering her face.

"Does making it back concern you so much?"

She shook her head. "I don't think so, but it's one of those things where I'm kind of on the fence about it. Sometimes I hate being so big that I can't take time off, but then I think to myself, this isn't everything that life is about. It's a double-edged sword."

He turned to face her. "With your social media presence, no one is going to wonder where you are or what you're doing. At this point, they're just as interested in what you and Garrett are doing together personally as they are what you're doing professionally. This is a whole new world, a whole new ballgame. Ain't nobody gonna forget Harmony Stewart."

Hannah laughed, throwing her head back. "That's right; 'cause we ain't gonna let 'em."

They hugged again before she made her way out of the studio. On this particular night, Shell had decided not to accompany her, so she quickly texted her to let her know they were done and she was getting a flight out of Nashville to Los Angeles. Her phone rang almost instantly.

"You're not even waiting until morning?" Shell asked, "It's almost nine at night."

"Which means it's seven there, and by the time I get

there, it'll be around midnight their time. I can sleep on the plane; it's not that big of a deal."

"What about clothes?"

Hannah was getting good and fed up with Shell trying to talk her out of anything that had to do with Garrett. "I packed a bag this morning, and I'd like for you to stop this."

"Stop what?"

The airport was less than twenty minutes from the studio, and Hannah was already halfway to the airport with her lead foot. "Being the way you're being."

"I don't know what you're talkin' about."

"You do," she insisted. "The thing with you is that you're fine as long as I check my schedule and get the okay from you on everything. I don't have to do that in my personal life. I'm going to see Garrett. The sound guys told me I have at least a week before they're done."

"There's a lot you could be doing around here. Photography and press."

"I can just as easily do that in California. Stop being a bitch." Hannah's voice was getting louder, and she pulled out a word she hardly ever used.

"What?"

"You are. I get that you're used to our relationship being the most important one in our lives, but it's not anymore. It's still important to me, but if you keep pushing me, I'm going to shut down, and then where will we be? Stop being so damn jealous."

Shell swallowed roughly. Like always, Hannah had called it right. She was jealous. Jealous of the fact that Hannah knew exactly what she wanted and that she had a man who knew what he wanted. They weren't scared to jump in blind and with both feet. She envied it and wanted it for herself.

"I'm sorry."

"While I'm gone, you need to figure out what it is you want. Do you still want to be my friend or just my assistant and partial manager? I can't keep doing this and I refuse to. I'll see ya in a few days." Hannah hung up as she pulled into Nashville International Airport.

She was done letting other people run her life. She'd told people that same thing a million times. At some point, they were going to believe her.

I'm here! Be aware, even at almost midnight, there's a bunch of paparazzi still here.

Hannah looked down at the text as she de-boarded the plane and made her way in the throng of people to the baggage claim. She'd texted Stacey once they were in the air to let her know that she was on her way, and to ask for a ride. While she recorded during the day, Black Friday recorded day and night. She knew that this was one night they were booked until the wee hours of the morning.

"Ugh, at least I had a little bit of sleep on the plane," she whispered to herself as she broached the concourse, seeing Stacey, but also seeing the paparazzi she had been talking about.

"Hey!" Stacey yelled, waving.

"Hey, yourself. I don't have any luggage, just this." She indicated the shoulder bag that she'd carried on.

"Then let's get the fuck outta here, these guys make me claustrophobic."

"Is there a huge star coming in today?" Hannah asked, the two of them keeping their head down and moving swiftly.

"Yeah, girl, you."

As Stacey said that, the paparazzi noticed her and Hannah moving quickly away from the throng, and she heard someone yell "Harmony" loudly. "Crap," she laughed, wondering if they should run.

They looked at each other, "I can't run as fast as Garrett," Stacey laughed.

"Me neither."

They locked hands as about twenty photographers crowded around them. Neither wanted to get separated from the other. Questions and comments were shouted from everywhere as the bright flash of cameras shined in their faces.

Harmony!! How is Reaper? Are you here to visit him? Trouble in paradise? Here to check on your hubby?

She kept her head down, moving forward, inch by inch. "Here to visit," she called out.

Is he pissed about the pictures of you and Bryson Grant taken outside the studio the other day? He couldn't have been happy! Was Bryson taking your wedding ring off?

That was a new one on her; she didn't know anything had been printed. Garrett hadn't mentioned it, so possibly he hadn't seen them. That would be a relief to her, especially since she hadn't seen them either.

"Can you guys give us a little bit of room, please?" she asked, finally lifting her head up.

The flashbulbs went off even faster.

C'mon, Harmony, smile for us! You and Stacey pose together. Give us something.

She did her best to smile, but when there were this many people around her and she couldn't see an escape, it made her feel uneasy. They were trying desperately to make their way to the end of the terminal so they could get out of the doors, but it was taking forever. Just as she was about to lose it, she felt a strong arm come around her shoulders and give her some breathing room. Looking up, she smiled at her father-in-law.

"Stacey brought me, just in case you two needed me. I figured when you didn't make it back to the car by a certain time, you needed me."

Garrett got his height and muscular build from his dad, and obviously a bit of his temper too as Kevin started yelling for the crush of photographers to give them some room. This time, they listened.

Finally they made it to the end of the terminal and out of the glass doors. Once they were there, she inhaled a deep breath of fresh air. "Thanks for coming to save us," she said as she hooked hands with Kevin. The three of them made a united front, finally running for the car.

They could hear the photographers giving chase behind them, but Stacey and Kevin had been smart and parked in a regulated area, so that the paparazzi couldn't follow.

"That's insane," Kevin shook his head.

"It is," Hannah agreed. "And honestly scary, when I don't have Garrett with me. He's big enough that he can give me some breathing room, but when it's only me or me and another friend like Stacey, they swarm everywhere. Nobody wants to get on Garrett's bad side, so when he's with me, it's not so bad. Thank you again."

"Not a problem," he told her as he backed the car out of the lot and then pulled into the main lane to get out of the airport.

She laughed, but it was humorless as they saw another group of photographers, racing to get pictures of her in the front seat of the car. They were too slow though as Kevin pulled the car onto the freeway.

"You want me to take you to the house or studio?"

Stacey, from where she sat in the back, spoke. "They still have a few hours at the studio."

"Then that's where I want to go. I still feel weird going into the house by myself. I know that's stupid, but I hate going in there without Garrett with me."

"I'll drop you off," Kevin told her as he continued driving. "This time of night, it shouldn't take us long to get to Huntington Beach."

She knew it was about an hour drive from the airport to the studio, but she'd never been to the studio before and she'd never seen Garrett in the studio. This would be a new experience and it was one that she couldn't wait to have.

Chapter Seven

"They're in the second room on the right," Stacey told Hannah as they pulled to a stop in front of the recording studio that Black Friday used.

"You aren't coming in?"

Stacey grinned. "Already been there tonight and got kicked out by big brother."

Hannah laughed loudly. That meant Stacey and Brad had been a little too close for Garrett's comfort. He was doing better with the two of them being together, as long as it wasn't thrown in his face. Every once in a while, he had to put a stop to it.

"Nobody should be at the front desk, but if they are, show them this," Stacey shoved a laminated card in her hand that at first looked like a backstage pass.

Hannah turned it over in her hand, examining it. It had her picture on it, her name, and at the bottom "Garrett's wife".

"Everybody who comes to the studio out here has one. They have to keep it on lockdown, because fans like to sneak in and their favorite line is that they're family. The band had these made last time they were in the studio. I snuck and had you one made today," she explained.

There was something about seeing her name. The card said Hannah Thompson—not Harmony Stewart, not Hannah Stewart. It said Hannah Thompson. She knew she was wearing a stupid grin on her face, but the fact of the matter was, she hadn't had time to change her last name and, in all honesty, hadn't really thought about it. Seeing it in print like that solidified what her plans were. She had to find a happy medium between Harmony, the singer, and Hannah, the wife. If that meant being less Harmony, then so be it. "Thank you so much, for everything, you two!"

"Not a problem." Kevin yawned from behind the wheel. "Garrett's been a big grouch lately, and I know it's because of the way the two of you have been seeing each other. Go enjoy your week with him. Maybe he can take a day or two off himself."

She hugged both of them as best she could before grabbing her purse and carry-on bag. When she got to the front door, she noticed there was a scanner and no other way to get in. Taking the badge that Stacey had given her, she swiped it, almost squealing when it let her in. She was so close to seeing Garrett she could taste it. Entering the building was eerie at this time of night—she glanced at her watch—or early morning, as the case may be. She walked down the hall to the room that Stacey had told her they would be in and noticed that it said Black Friday on the outside of the door. The dilemma was if she should knock or not, but that was settled for her when the door opened and she came face to face with Jared.

"Well, well, well. Look what the cat dragged in." He grinned at her, scooping her up in a hug.

Over the past few months, the two of them had developed a friendship that bordered on brother and sister. She was equally excited to see him, squealing when he swung her around her in a circle.

"Who are you molesting? Is that Shell?"

Hannah bit back the laugh. If Garrett only knew. But she and Jared were hidden by the partially open door.

"Should we mess with him a bit?" he asked, an evil twinkle in his eye.

"No, I can't wait to see him!" She moved back to allow Jared to come out of the room. He had obviously been on a mission to go somewhere when she had appeared.

"I think you should come see," Jared called over his shoulder before walking across the hall to the restroom.

"Who the fuck…" Garrett's words were cut off when he saw who stood in front of him.

They stared at each other for what seemed like a year, until the side of his mouth kicked up, giving her that half-grin that made every part of her body stand at attention. He didn't take his green eyes off her as he turned his head slightly. "I'll be right back."

He quickly slammed the door and then grabbed her hand, leading her down another hallway, this one darker than the one they had stood in before. No words were spoken between them as he stopped and pushed her up against the wall. One hand boxed her in, along with his body, while the other cupped the back of her neck.

Hannah's heart pounded in her chest, and she could hear the breath coming from her mouth. It sounded like she had just run a marathon. He adjusted his stance so that he was more on eye level with her. It unnerved her because he still hadn't said anything. Her hands went to his sides, gripping his shirt, unsure of what to do.

"I missed you," he whispered, a moment before his lips captured hers.

This was one of the things that she loved about him. Sometimes with them it was a slow burn, a casual build up. Other times it was a 100 mph rush to the finish line. This was one of those times. His lips owned her, manipulating her mouth into doing exactly what he wanted her to. The hand at the back of her neck applied gentle pressure, shifting her whichever way he wanted her to go, and she followed him, never hesitating. When her tongue snaked out, touching his, he let his body fall against hers, pressing her even harder against the wall, his breath coming as fast as hers. She could feel the pounding of his heart against her chest.

"Fuck, Han, I missed you," he growled out again as he ripped his lips from hers.

She could do nothing more than nod as she wrapped her arms around his neck, lifting her chin up to make room when he moved his mouth along the column of her throat. Her knees were getting weak from the feelings coursing through her body, and she wasn't sure that she could remain standing for much longer.

As with everything else, he was right there with her. "I got you," he rasped against her shoulder. He'd somehow pulled her T-shirt down, exposing a part of her shoulder and chest to him. His large hands sat at her hips. Bending his knees, he lifted, wrapping her legs around his waist, using the wall for leverage. "I got you, always got you" he said again, going back to the skin he had exposed.

Her mind was swirling from the feelings he evoked in her. She dug her fingers into his hair, tugging tightly, not wanting him to let her go, not wanting him to move his lips from her body. But she wanted a turn too. Maneuvering so that she could get to him, she allowed herself to play. Under the cover of the dark hallway, with people not too far away, she sucked his earlobe into her mouth, feeling the coolness of the earring he wore there. She felt his fingers grip her harder, grinding himself against her.

She wasn't sure how long they stood there, making out like a couple of high school kids, but eventually Garrett pulled away, burying his head in her neck. His breath tickled against the skin there, but she panted just as hard as he did.

"I can't." He shook his head. "If we keep going, I'll have to go home and change my pants," he said darkly, next to her ear.

Hannah couldn't hold back the giggle that erupted, and she was glad for the darkness of the hallway—it hid her blush. It was fun to play with him. She bit her lip, thrusting herself against him.

"Shit, woman." His head dropped against her shoulder and his fingers tightened at her hips. "I'm trying to get myself under control here."

"Maybe I like you out of control," she whispered, speaking for the first time.

He laughed, using his teeth to nip at the skin he had exposed earlier. "You just like to tease me."

"I do, but I also like the follow-through." She lifted

his chin so that she could see his face. "There's that face I missed."

He breathed deeply before adjusting his stance again and slowly lowering her down so that her feet touched the floor. "What are you doing here? I didn't even know you were coming."

She continued to hold his hand as they talked, not wanting to lose that connection with him. For some reason she wanted to touch him, didn't want to break it. "I got done recording, and the other things I have planned, I can do here." She shrugged. "I'm here for a little over a week, as long as you want me."

"I think I've proven that I want you forever, babe." He reached down, moving her hair back from her face. "We still have another hour here. You wanna come in or do you want to take my car home?"

"Come in." She gripped his hand tightly in excitement. "I've never seen you in the studio before. It's a new experience for me."

He loved that she got so excited over the little things. It helped keep him grounded in the world that sometimes got to be way too serious. He appreciated it, and it always reminded him that he had made the best decision of his life when he got her to marry him. A thought occurred to him out of nowhere. "Is Shell with you, or is she coming tomorrow?"

"I don't know what Shell's doing. I think she's staying home."

The way she said the words caused him to closely study her face. "Everything okay with her?"

"Yes and no. She's having a hard time not being my only best friend anymore. She and I are having some growing pains, but we'll get through it. I told her she needs to figure out where she wants to be in my life."

Garrett could understand that. As he had gotten older, many of his friendships had changed and evolved. It just happened. "Are you okay with that?"

"I am." She nodded. There was no reason for her to go into the real reason they'd had an argument. She was sick to death of dealing with the duet that was never going to be.

"If you're good, then I'm good. C'mon, let's go finish this real quick. That way we can get home."

She loved every time that he called it home. Wherever he was, it was home for her, and she hoped it was the same way for him.

They walked down the hallway, and he pushed open the door that she had attempted to go in a few minutes before. "Look who's here."

Hannah was greeted by all of them enthusiastically. It made her happy that they made the effort to do that because she knew that Garrett being married was a new thing for all of them too. "Thanks," she told them, accepting a hug from Brad.

"You're in luck," the sound engineer told her. "Garrett's about to go lay down some tracks. You'll get to hear him fuck up a million times."

Everyone in the room laughed, calling out insults to their front man while he held up two middle fingers.

She giggled. "So mean!"

"I know, right?" Garrett put his hand over his heart. "It's a good thing you're here. I'll need you to stroke my ego the way these guys like to shoot it down."

"Or something else," another person called out causing more laughs.

This was a group of total guys, and she could already tell that they were raunchy and perverted. She had been around roadies for a long time; no matter how she goodie two-shoes she acted, hardly anything fazed her. "That'll be a little later," she grinned. Turning, she had a seat next to Jared and clapped him on the thigh. "I'm just gonna have a seat next to your BFF here and enjoy the show."

The twinkle in her eye made him wonder exactly she had in mind.

Chapter Eight

Hannah checked the time on her cell phone and had to smirk. This was different. It was almost one in the afternoon and she and Garrett were cooking breakfast. She hadn't even been aware that he knew his way around the kitchen. With anyone else, this would have felt weird. He wore no shirt and a pair of boxers; she wore only a shirt that barely covered her behind. With him, though, she felt comfortable. It had been a very long time coming.

"In all the times we've been together, you've never cooked!" she accused him, looking behind her as she cut up strawberries and apples.

He shrugged as he flipped the omelet over in the skillet. "I have to be in the mood, and I was fucking starving when I woke up."

She couldn't hide the smile on her face, and he smiled widely back at her. Both of them thinking about the early morning they'd had together. Her stomach picked that moment to growl, and he laughed.

"Sounds like you're fucking starving too."

"Possibly." Her answer was coy as she turned back

around.

Out of the blue, his hand connected with the bare skin that her underwear didn't cover.

"Ouch! Garrett!"

His face turned serious for a moment. "That's for not telling me about those pictures of you and Bryson."

She was subdued for a moment. "It was nothing," she told him as she turned around, putting the plate of fruit on the table and having a seat.

"If I didn't trust and know you, they wouldn't look like nothing," he told her carefully as he took a large bite of the food that sat in front of him.

Hannah also took a bite, chewing slowly. She wasn't sure how to approach this because she still hadn't seen the pictures that everyone was talking about. "I haven't seen them."

Green eyes cut over to her and Garrett's face was stormy as he pulled his iPad over to where he sat and tapped a few buttons. She was not going to feel guilty about this. She had done nothing wrong, and just because people had gotten pictures and they looked bad, it didn't mean anything. When he pushed the iPad over, she grabbed it with both hands and had a look.

"This totally isn't what it looks like," she whispered. He had been right, they did look awful. In one, Bryson had hold of her hand and was inspecting her engagement ring, and she was glancing up at him. From the angle the pictures were taken at, it almost appeared to be an adoring look.

"I know." He cleared his throat as the sound came out rough. "I know," he said again, this time more sure. "But it doesn't feel good to know you've been arguing with your wife and the subject of that argument is taking pictures like that with her. To know that he's there and you're not. There's a part of it that not only hurts, but makes you angry too. I had to go through the stages, but I'm good now."

"He was talking about how different my engagement ring is. If they would have waited a few seconds, they would have seen me jerk my hand away from his." She stabbed a strawberry and crammed it into her mouth. "See, this is why I want my break. This is what makes me question the career path I've chosen."

Garrett sighed. "I don't want you giving something up for me. Both of us know that it's just a knee-jerk reaction right now."

She wasn't so sure. In every thought she had in her head, it came back to her wanting to be a wife and eventually a mother. The ache to be with him all the time gnawed at her belly. "I'm going to fulfill what I told them I would, but after this small tour, I *am* taking some time off. The only way I'm gonna know whether it's a knee-jerk reaction is if I give it the proper amount of time. If I'm bored in a few weeks, then I know it was knee-jerk, but if I'm having a good time, then I'll know it's what I needed. I've got to try it out."

He nodded, taking a drink of the water he had sitting beside his plate. "I don't want you to regret this." He held up his left hand, indicating the ring he was wearing.

"Seriously?" She almost laughed. "I'm not ever gonna regret that. That's the best thing I've ever done."

"I just think that you're young, ya know?" He trailed off.

"I am young, but I know what I want. I wouldn't

have gone through with it if it wasn't what I wanted. I'm sorry that those pictures made you question that."

They were quiet as they ate their breakfast. This had been exactly what Hannah had wanted to avoid, why she wanted this off time to be normal. If they were any other married couple, no one would think a thing about those pictures. The last thing she wanted was for Garrett to question her. When there were questions, the relationship suffered.

"I'm not mad, I trust you," he told her.

"I'm glad. If I had known that would happen, I wouldn't have run out of the studio. They made me so angry, continually asking me to do that duet with him. I just needed some breathing room, and then you and I got into an argument, and there he was asking me what was wrong. It was a horrible series of events."

He nodded, taking the last bite of the omelet on his plate. "We have a few hours before we have to hit the studio, what do you say we go take Havock out to the beach?"

The dog, having heard his name, got up, whining as he walked over to the table. Hannah grinned, leaning down to pet him. "I think that's a great idea."

"Are you wearing that because the last time we were here, that picture started all kinds of ruckus with us?" Garrett asked as they strolled along the beach, hand in hand. Havock ran in front of them, picking up a ball that Garrett had thrown and bringing it back to them.

Hannah glanced down at her outfit, cut-off jean

shorts and a tank top, and laughed. "I honestly didn't even think about it, but maybe. It's funny, and I haven't even talked to you about this, but I've started wearing tighter clothes, just so the paparazzi can see I'm either not pregnant, or still the same weight that I was when they took that unflattering shot."

He grimaced. "Yeah, that whole pregnancy thing was kind of annoying."

For the first two months of their marriage, there had been two stories running—that Hannah was pregnant and that's why they'd gotten married so quickly and then that she'd had a miscarriage, which was why a baby bump was never seen.

"I agree, it really hurts my feelings that they can play around with the words miscarriage and pregnant like that, but it is what it is."

"I like that you say that now. You don't get all uptight and freaked out so much anymore."

She shrugged, stopping a moment to bend down and get the ball that Havock had dropped at their feet. "It's like when you put a ring on my finger, I felt at peace. I can't explain it."

"It happened like that for me too."

The smile on her face was bright as she reached back and threw the ball for the dog, laughing as it didn't go very far at all. Havock looked back at her and took off at a much slower run than he had when Garrett had thrown it.

"He disapproves of your throw, babe. He looked back at you like, 'really?'"

She laughed. "I know, I can't help it. That hurt to throw that far."

"Bring it over here, buddy." Garrett tapped his thigh.

"He's never going to drop it at my feet again," she giggled as Havock chanced a second glance at her, disappointment in his eyes.

"That's okay; you give him cuddles, all day, every day." He grunted as he threw it extra hard.

"Oh, now you're just showin' off."

"I was letting him get one more nice run in because we've got to go back to the house and change. I've got to be at the studio in an hour."

She glanced up at him, shielding her eyes in the late day sunlight, even though she wore sunglasses. "Is it okay for me to come with you tonight?"

"If you want to, I am more than happy to have you out. I just don't want you to get bored. You got finished with your own shit a few days ago."

"Yeah." She gripped his hand tighter. "But it's different watching you. It's almost like I look at it through different eyes."

They were quiet for a minute until she sighed.

"What's wrong?" he asked.

"I don't want to beat a dead horse, but I've gotta know that you're okay with those pictures. You kinda glossed over it earlier."

"They do piss me off." The honesty was blatant in his voice. "But what kind of a man would I be if I took those pictures at face value after I preached to you about the picture of you being 'fat'." He made quotation marks with his fingers.

"You're still mad about it?"

"I'm mad at the fact they used Shell to get to you. Then they play with your head. That's what pisses me off."

"I asked them if they would contact your record company so that we could sing together. We'll have to see what they say."

Garrett had a pretty good idea of what his record company would say, but he realized that he could always hope for the best. "They haven't contacted me, or management, so maybe they haven't made a decision on what they're going to do yet."

"I hope they say yes. I would love to sing with you." She put her arms around his waist and hugged him tight, burying her head in his chest.

"I would love to sing with you too. Maybe we should see if we can get an Instagram campaign going. You know something like hashtag Harmony and Reaper Duet?"

"That's an awesome idea." She laughed against his shirt.

"Okay, we really gotta go."

"Fine," she sighed. "Let's go see you be all sexy while you work."

His face burned bright. "Yes, let's do that."

They walked towards the house, Havock following closely behind. Hannah looked behind her, hoping to get one more look at the ocean before they had to be cooped up in the studio for the rest of the night. Sweeping along the coast was a dark cloud; she could see rain coming down. Shaking her head, she hoped it wasn't an omen of what was to come.

Chapter Nine

As Hannah listened to the amount of opinions being thrown out, she had to shake her head. This experience was making her very glad that she was a solo artist. The guys were knee-deep in a discussion about whether the song they had just spent over four hours recording was going to work or not, and there were four very different opinions.

"What do you think, Hannah?" the sound engineer asked, obviously sick of hearing the guys go back and forth. He wore an exasperated look on his face.

"Ohhh, no, no, no." She shook her head, looking up from her phone, where she had been texting with Shell. They were working on getting their friendship back on track. "I'm not getting in the middle of this."

"You're a fan, aren't you? You were one before you met and married Garrett, what do you think?"

She gave him the evil eye for throwing her under the bus like this, because now, she had four sets of eyes staring intently at her. "I think that I'm a fan, but I'm too close to the situation to be objective."

They all began talking, this time at her.

"C'mon, babe. Whatever you have to say, whether it is a popular opinion or not, might make us decide what we need to do," Garrett told her.

She knew that she shouldn't do this, but she was sick of hearing them fight, and they had been doing it for too long. She wanted to get out of here and spend some more time with her husband. Carefully, she bit her lip, considering how she needed to say this. "If you're wanting to move away from your old sound, then you're not doing it with this song."

"So you're saying it's too much like our old stuff?" Brad pumped his fist in the air. He'd been arguing that.

She nodded, cutting her dark eyes over to where Garrett sat. She was going against his opinion, and she hoped he could respect that. He gazed openly at her, but nodded as their eyes met.

"I'm beating a dead horse?" he questioned.

"You are. You wanted this one to be different, and while it is, it's not different enough. Not in my opinion. It sounds like a watered-down version of the music that all the fans love."

He smirked at her. "Damn, baby, just tell me what you really think."

The room laughed because she had.

"But you guys do what you want," she quickly added. "I mean, it's your record, it's not mine, and it's not the fans. It's yours."

Her alarm on her phone went off, and she sighed. She had hoped they would be done by now. "I hate do this to you guys, but I've got to go meet with the photographer and take some shots for my new promo pictures and stuff."

"You going by yourself?" Garrett asked. It was going on seven at night, and while it wasn't unusual for shoots to be done at night, he didn't want her going by herself. Especially given that this photographer was a man.

"Nope," she smiled. "Stacey's coming with, but I've got to get out of here if I'm gonna have time to pick her up."

She said her goodbyes, kissing her husband on the cheek before she left. As she always did before she drove in California traffic, she sat in the car for a few minutes, giving herself a pep talk. This would all be okay.

"You want me to wear what?" Hannah glanced at the outfit the stylist held up, trying to keep her eyes from popping out of her head.

"You'll look hot in it, and you're the wife of a rocker now. You can pull it off. Besides, I listened to some of the new stuff. It definitely has a more rocking sound to it, a harder edge. You're a gorgeous woman, embrace it."

This stylist was insane, Hannah was sure of that. Shaking her head, she took the outfit into the dressing room and began putting it on. This type of look had never been her thing, but maybe she needed to expand. Maybe now that she was married, she wouldn't mind looking sexy.

"C'mon, Han, it's just an outfit," she told herself, disrobing.

Fishnet stockings were something she'd never once in her life worn before this moment, but she dutifully pulled them over her bare legs. Same with the leather miniskirt. She turned around; checking herself out in the mirror, making sure everything was covered. One wrong move and she would be showing parts of herself that she only wanted Garrett to see, but it looked good, if she did say so herself. Grabbing the clothing pack that the stylist had given her, she pulled out a hot pink bra and had to blink at the brightness of it.

"Wow," she laughed.

Once that was on, she grinned slightly as a thought popped into her head. She grabbed her cell phone and took a picture in the mirror, sending it to Garrett. She felt a little evil and wondered what he would have to say about this. Next, she grabbed what appeared to be a black tank top, along with a cropped motorcycle jacket. The tank top came down low, showing the top of the hot pink lace, and the motorcycle jacket covered up the gaping holes in the side.

Looking at herself, she had to admit that she did like it. The stylist had done her hair in corkscrew curls, and her makeup was dark to match the outfit. Her cell made a noise, and she bent down to pick it up from where she had dropped it.

Please tell me you're wearing a fucking shirt, and can you, for the love of all that's holy, wear that home? Especially after you sided with everyone else during our conversation about the new song.

She threw her head back, laughing loudly. Leave it to her husband to get to the heart of all he really wanted to know. She quickly texted back that she wasn't sure if they would give her the clothing from this shoot.

Normally they did, but she didn't want to make it that easy on him.

"You ready, Harmony?" the stylist asked from outside the door.

"Give me just a sec," she yelled back as she put on the stiletto heels they'd also given her. A deep breath fortified her courage, and she stepped out. "How does it look?" she turned around in a circle.

"Hot. I'm glad you let me do what I wanted to do with you. You have such great muscle tone; it shows you aren't afraid to eat, and that's sexy. Thank you," the other woman grinned.

Hannah didn't know if she was being hit on or not, so she smiled back and walked towards the photography set. The guys in attendance, along with Stacey, whistled loudly. She blushed but turned in a circle and did a curtsy anyway. "Thank you! You're great for a girl's self-esteem."

"We ready to get to work?"

She nodded. "We are, Damien."

He was one of the top music photographers at the moment, and she was more than excited to work with him. It wasn't easy to get an appointment, but he was a huge Black Friday fan and saw it as an honor to shoot Reaper's wife. She would take it however she could get it, and if that meant using her wedding ring, she would. Garrett had laughed when she told him that.

"Okay, Harmony, give me heat," he told her as he directed her on how to sit. This time it was with her legs crossed, her arms propped up behind her. Damien stood on a ladder, shooting her from over top.

She turned her head to the side, a slow smile spreading over her face as she saw Garrett standing next to Stacey. His tattooed arms were held in front of his chest, and she could see that his muscles bulged slightly against the tightness of the T-shirt.

"That's it Harmony, that's what I want to see," Damien encouraged her.

Garrett's eyes met hers, and she was pretty sure that the temperature in the room went up about thirty degrees. Her arms were getting tired, so she casually let herself drop to her elbows, turning her head so that she now looked at the camera. She threw her head back, exposing her throat. If she closed her eyes, she could imagine that Garrett was right there with her, and it made it easier to turn on the heat that Damien wanted so badly.

"You're gorgeous," he told her, as he snapped away. "Can you arch your back, just a little, not overly so. We're not going for pornographic here."

She giggled, opening her eyes as she did her best to arch her back in the way that he was describing.

"There, that's great, I love that little look of mischief you have. Keep going, you're a natural."

It was easy to pose for his pictures, because he knew exactly what to say to her, and it didn't make her self-conscious. She wished she'd had him on every photo shoot from the last four years.

"Okay, just need a few more shots," he told her. Glancing to the side, he spotted Reaper. "You think we can get your husband in on these?"

They had never really done pictures together that were posed, except for their wedding pictures, and those had been done quickly. She would love to do this with him. Crooking her finger at him, she beckoned him over. "You wanna pose for a few with me?

"In that outfit? Fuck yes," he answered, grinning brightly.

They called a makeup person over who gave him a quick touchup, and then he had a seat on the prop that Hannah had been leaning against.

"Okay, Harmony, I want you to stand in front of him with your back to his chest. I want some romance, you two are newlyweds."

Garrett clasped one of her hands at her stomach and then carefully placed one hand at her thigh, slightly pushing the skirt up. It wasn't indecent, but it still caused Hannah's breath to catch. She could feel the heat coming from his body, and she couldn't help but look partially behind her shoulder at him, closing her eyes.

"That's it, you two, pretend like I'm not even here," Damien told them as he continued snapping away.

Hannah's eyes lowered as she saw him moving in closer to her. She felt the slight brush of his lips against the back of her neck and smiled slowly, using her other hand to clasp it around his thigh.

They were lost in their own little world as they continued to touch each other, sometimes softly, sometimes with more force. Garrett whispered words into her ear, causing her to blush and giggle, and at some point, she turned so that she sat on his lap. It was the most fun she'd had with him in front of someone who wasn't a part of their inner circle.

All too soon, Damien stopped snapping and laughed at the two of them. "You're gonna explode my camera lens. You can definitely tell the two of you have chemistry. Thank you for sharing it with me."

"Hey, man, can you send me some of those?" Garrett asked, his voice quieter than normal.

"Sure thing. You have a gorgeous wife, and together the two of you are smoking. I would love to photograph you for an art magazine if either of you are ever interested. Just keep it in mind."

They both nodded as they made their way off set.

"I kinda feel like he's asking us to do a porno," Garrett whispered.

She laughed so hard she snorted before going into the dressing room and changing back into her street clothes.

"Don't forget to bring that outfit home with ya. We might make it our own," he reminded her.

In answer, she threw the bra over the door at him, smirking when he whistled. Coming out here and spending time with him was one of the best decisions she had ever made.

Chapter Ten

"I can't believe I'm leaving tomorrow."

Hearing those words come from Hannah's mouth cut Garrett to the core. He couldn't believe their time was already at an end. It felt like this revolving door was never going to stop, and he had to keep himself from going to a place he knew he wouldn't be able to pull back from. Being pissed on her last night in California would not do either of them any good. He wanted to have good memories to get him through the long eight weeks that would follow.

"Me neither."

It was hard to fathom that she wouldn't be lying here in this exact spot with him tomorrow night. They were on the balcony, spread out on the lounger there. He could hear the ocean and knew if he bothered to open his eyes, he would be able to see the moon reflecting off of the water.

"You sure you're not going to get in trouble for not recording tonight?" she asked as she snuggled closer, sighing when his arms tightened around her.

"Really don't give a fuck if they're mad. I told them

you're leaving tomorrow. I figure they should know what the hell that means."

They were quiet for a few minutes before she cleared her throat. "As soon as I get back to Nashville, I'm going to be running around like a chicken with my head cut off. I start tour rehearsals the day after tomorrow. I heard from Shell today, they approved the CD and the photography that Damien took. They're moving forward with releasing at the end of the month, and then the first full week of October, I go on tour."

He worried about her, that she was pushing herself and it was for him. "I don't want you to kill yourself with this schedule."

She sighed. "I keep thinking that once it's over, I get a full year and a half with you. It's worth it. You know being tired and rundown is a part of this business and it's something that we can't help most of the time. I'll be tired everyday if it means I can spend more time with you."

When she spoke those words, it gutted him. It felt like he wasn't going the extra mile like she did. "I hate that if feel like you put more into this marriage than I do. It makes me feel like a shitty husband and less of a man," he admitted.

"It's easier for me. I don't have to clear my schedule with three other people. I can make my own decisions without getting it cleared, for the most part, and then when I'm ready to go, I only have to get one or two plane tickets. I don't mind making the sacrifice. Besides," she kissed his jawline, "you surprise me all the time. This isn't going to be permanent."

Everything she said, he knew as true, but it didn't

make the situation any easier in his eyes. "Fuckin' hate this."

"Don't be a Negative Nathan on our last night together for a while. We both knew what we were getting into when we decided to do this. We either work at it or we let it fall apart."

"Talk about a role reversal." He grinned at her. "Usually I'm the one telling you to let it go."

She shrugged, smirking. "I'm workin' on it." She turned serious. "What's going on with you? You're never like this."

"I don't know." He ran his hand through his hair. It was getting longer now that they were recording. It was kind of a superstitious thing that he didn't cut it while they were in the studio. "I have a bad feeling and I don't know why, I don't know what about. I just don't want you to get on that plane and go away from me tomorrow."

"I have to, Garrett." She kissed his neck sweetly. "I don't have a choice."

"I wish I was rich enough to buy you out of your contract."

Hannah laughed. "That would be awesome, if we even had that much money together. I'm sure if we sold our houses, cars, and got all of our stock options together that we could. I don't want to quit forever though, just for a few years to experience life. Who knows, maybe I won't want to go back to it and we'll have to see what can be done. We don't know the future."

She was right, they didn't know the future, but he knew that he didn't want to let her go. He didn't want to spend the next eight weeks trying to find five minutes here and there to call her. Knowing that they didn't have a choice didn't make it better.

"It's because I've been here," she whispered. "It's always harder when you leave me. I cry for hours, especially after I take you the airport."

"You seem fine, every damn time," he accused.

"What good is it to let you know how bad it tears me up, when you have no choice? All it would do would be to make you feel like crap. I don't want that for you, so I hold it together until you get on the plane and I get out to my car. It's hard and it gets harder every time. It is what it is. We can't change it right now, no matter how much we both might want to."

"This sucks," he laughed. "We're both at the top of our games in our own musical genres, and our asses have to go and fall in love."

"We can't help when we fall in love."

He allowed her to clasp their hands together and entwine their fingers. In truth, he loved when she held his hand like that; it made him feel more connected to her. "I'm sorry that I'm having such a girl moment. This isn't like me at all."

"I know that too, but at the same time, we've had a heck of a lot happen to us since we met. We've not known each other for a year yet and we're already married. You have to admit, we've done things at a crazy pace."

Slinging his arm around her neck, he pulled her to him, burying his face in her hair and breathing deeply. "Eight weeks, right?"

"Eight weeks," she confirmed. "Eight more weeks

and then I'm with you for over a year. It's been approved, I've executed my clause, and nothing can stop it, not even legal action. This is mine to do with what I want. What I want is to follow you around and be your own personal groupie," she giggled.

"My own personal groupie, huh?" he raised his eyebrows.

"I've never been a groupie before, but I would love to be yours." She giggled again.

He couldn't tell if she was being serious or not, so he decided to see what she would do. Instead of bemoaning the fact that she wouldn't be here, he wanted to bury himself inside of her and forget about what they had to face. Garrett licked his lips and lowered his voice. "If you were my groupie, I'd have you bent over that table over there." He pointed to the coffee table that sat where he sometimes used his laptop.

She cocked her head to the side, not sure if she understood what he was saying to her. "You would, huh?"

"I would." He nodded, but didn't say anything else. He wanted her to make the decision on her own, if she wanted to do this or not. He had to admit, he'd often wondered what it would be like to have her the way he'd had other women, but he was scared to tell her that. He didn't want her to think less of him.

Hannah bit her bottom lip, contemplating if she wanted to do what he was obviously suggesting. It could be fun, and it would definitely make for a memorable last night in California. She wore a tank top and a skirt from where they had gone to dinner with his family earlier. Her brown eyes met his green ones. There she could see that he wanted her to do this, but he wouldn't pressure her. He wanted this to be her decision and not his. If they were going to do this, it was going to be because she wanted to.

Disentangling herself from his arms, she stood up and kicked her shoes off before walking over towards the table. Once she got there, she looked over her shoulder at him. "Is this where you want me?" The harsh breath that she heard from him was enough to convince her that she wanted to do this; she loved to see his control slip, even if it wasn't fully.

"Down on your knees and face forward," he told her.

Hannah could hear him behind her as she kneeled. He had gotten up off the lounger and was walking towards her. She closed her eyes, wanting to experience this fully. She could feel the heat from his body as he came up directly behind her. Goosebumps appeared on her arms and her nipples hardened as she heard him work the belt that he wore then the slip of his zipper; even the sound of the material of his pants dropping caused moisture to pool at her core. This was exciting her way more than she'd thought it would. After a moment, she heard him lower so that he was also on his knees, but even on his knees he was much taller and bigger than she was.

Hannah shivered when he moved the hair back from her neck and then attacked the side with his mouth, nipping and biting the skin there. Tipping her head back slightly, she gave him more room to work, the invitation to take it a step further. Her mouth opened as she felt his long fingers tangle in her hair and exert pressure, pulling it back further for him.

"You like this?" he questioned as his other hand slid down her neck, stopping to cup her breast before moving further down her body. His fingers played with the hem of her skirt at her thigh before diving under. "You didn't answer me."

Hannah couldn't. Her throat felt like it had closed, and all she could do was nod and make noises. She reached out and gripped the table hard as his hand encountered the barrier of her panties. He pushed them aside and she moaned.

"Answer me, or you don't get it."

"Yes," she whispered. "I like it."

He groaned then, removing his hand from where it was and moving it to her hip. He toyed with the string of her underwear there, before flexing his wrist and yanking, ripping them off her in the process. The next moment he was pushing on the back of her head.

"Bend."

His command was terse, and when she didn't follow through quickly enough, he layered his strong body over hers, pressing her against the coolness of the table. His hands went to her side where her arms lay and grabbed them, stretching her across the surface and then curled her fingers around the edge. "You hold on here," he instructed, his breath hot against her ear.

She nodded, not sure if he wanted her to speak. It didn't matter anymore when he plunged hard into her, causing a sound she'd never heard from herself to rip forth out of her throat. She heard a similar one come from his.

"It doesn't last long with groupies," he warned, his voice deep and dark in her ear. "I only care about one thing and that's getting off, but with you, I'll make sure you get yours too." He licked the edge of her ear, nipping at her earlobe.

Hannah wasn't sure she could handle this, the feelings that were coursing through her body. He owned her; it wasn't sweet, it wasn't intense like normal, this was more animalistic than anything she had ever felt before in her life. "Reaper," she breathed out, the choppiness making it sound like it was ripped from her body.

"What did you say?" he asked, his fingers digging into her hip, bringing her fully flush with his body.

"Reaper," she moaned again.

It was as if her calling him Reaper in that moment caused something to break inside him. He hauled her up from the table and plastered her back against his chest, never stopping the rhythmic thrusting into her body. Without warning he felt his body tighten and knew that it was going to be over, he couldn't stand having his wife like this. She trusted him, more than he ever thought she would, and it did things to him, things that he couldn't control. "Sorry," he apologized as he pumped inside her body, biting her neck when the feelings became too much.

Her breath was heavy as she felt the warmth spill out of him and into her body. She needed more, and she needed it now.

"I got you." His hand trailed from her hip to where they were joined.

"Feels good," she told him, her bottom lip between her teeth. Her hand trailed down her body and pressed his harder into her.

"Show me how you want it."

She pressed his hand harder into her, pumping her hips against the touch there, going after what she wanted. "Faster," she breathed.

He complied with her request, using his other hand to palm her chin and tip her neck back so that he had free reign. When his lips landed at the sensitive spot where her neck and shoulder joined, she lost it. Thrusting against him, she dug the nails of her other hand in his forearm where she had been holding on.

"You okay?" he chuckled, minutes later when their breathing had almost returned to normal.

"I think I'd like to be your groupie again sometime," she giggled.

"Anytime you want, baby. You're the best groupie I ever had."

Chapter Eleven

"I think you need to switch up that line right there," Shell told Hannah as they sat at the soundstage, rehearsing for her upcoming tour that would start in a few days.

"With the one before it?" Hannah asked. "It was an ad-lib to begin with, but I think you're right, it sounds a little forced." She reached down and made a note on the paper she had in front of her. "If y'all want to stop for lunch, I'm good with that."

Everyone agreed that they could use a short break, and Hannah took the opportunity to have a seat next to Shell.

"You would never know that you have a CD coming out today. You don't even look nervous."

"I am, oh trust me, I am. Did you not hear me getting up every hour last night?"

"I thought so, but you know how I sleep, I figured it was just me having those weird dreams," Shell laughed.

"No, it was me. I called Garrett like five times last night, and each time, he answered, even though I could tell he was tired. So I stopped calling him."

Shell glanced at her friend and could see the dark
circles under her eyes. It was obvious she'd had a hard
night. "Been a long couple of weeks, hasn't it?"

Hannah nodded, tears in her eyes. "Spending that
long stretch with him made this harder. I was afraid that
it would, but I didn't think it would be this much
harder."

"I'm sorry about all the shit I've been putting you
through," Shell blurted out.

Hannah shook her head. "What do you mean? I
don't understand."

"You know," Shell sighed. "When you first met
Garrett, I knew he was it for you, because I know you
don't give up your heart easily, I know you don't let
people in easily, and I know your feelings aren't
superficial. When you have them, they are yours and they
are genuine. I knew right then that I would be second in
your life."

"Shell..."

"No, give me a second. That was hard," she smiled.
"Because we've been all each other had for so long. I
was always the person that you deflected to. I helped you
make decisions and I helped you navigate through this
crazy life that the two of us lead. It was weird for me
when you got married and I was no longer the person
that you asked those questions of. I was a bitch about
the house, and I'm sorry. You were right."

"You are one of my best friends in this world,"
Hannah told her, hugging her around the neck. "But you
have to make room for Garrett. I want nothing more
than for you to love him the way you love me. I want
you to coexist with him, not make it difficult for me to

spend time with my husband."

"I get that now. Jared yelled at me over it."

"Jared yelled at you over that?" Hannah giggled. "How did he know?"

Shell blushed. "Oh, I went to him, all pissed off at you and spouting off about what a brat you were and how you were all up Garrett's ass and all this other stuff. He got mad at me and said exactly what you said. That I was being a bitch, and at some point, I had to let you make your own decisions. I'm sorry."

"I can't believe Jared said that to you." She laughed, holding her hand over her mouth.

"Well believe it, sister, because he did."

"I do agree that maybe I could have decided to go about telling you the changes I wanted to make in a different way, but I didn't know how to approach it, and I surely didn't want you angry with me. As long as you're still my BFF, I'm good. I don't want the marriage to ruin the friendship."

"It's not going to," Shell assured her. "I know my place now."

Hannah shook her head. "No, I never, ever wanted you to know your place. I hate how that sounds."

"I don't mean it the way you're taking it. I'm saying I realize that I still have a place, it's just not where it was before."

The two of them lapsed into a comfortable silence before Shell winked. "You are still giving me the house, though, right? Cause I totally have plans for your room."

"Oh my God." Hannah shook her head. "Yeah, we're still looking for a house. I actually found one that I love last night online. I'm hoping that Garrett and I can go tour it soon. I contacted the agent last night, but he's aware that we might have to tour it separately."

"I hate that for you, that so much of your firsts are separate."

"It's the life that we chose to live." Hannah glanced at her wedding ring and pushed it around on her finger. She wanted to call him but knew that with the time difference, he wasn't yet awake.

"Still sucks. Jared and I go through it a little, but we both know that if I wanted off, I could request it and you would let me do it."

Hannah opened her mouth to answer but stopped when she noticed a delivery man with what looked to be two dozen roses. "Can we help you?"

"I'm looking for Hannah Thompson," he read from the card.

Not many people called her by her married name, so she wondered who had sent her this bouquet. "That's me." She stood up, pulling her hair behind her in a loose ponytail.

"If you could just sign here, these are for you, ma'am."

She smiled when he called her ma'am. "Thank you so much. Your momma raised you with good manners."

He blushed and handed her the vase. "She did raise me up right. Congrats on all your success."

"Thank you," she called as he left, searching for the card he had read off of. "Now who sent these to me?" Once she found it, she pulled it out of the bouquet and sat the flowers down on the ground, opening the envelope.

Hey babe!

Congrats on the #1 on iTunes! FaceTime me later so we can talk!

Love,
Garrett

"It's from the hubby, and he said I'm the top spot on iTunes right now. I haven't even thought to check all day. I know that's crazy, but you know I've been all about this rehearsal."

Shell was already on her phone. "Damn, girlie! He's right! Congratulations!"

"Thank you." Hannah grinned, a bright smile on her face. She never expected any success, so when she got it, it was all the more exciting for her. "I wasn't sure how well it would do since we did almost zero promotion."

"The name Harmony Stewart is an auto-buy for most people, and your fans are amazing. They don't need months of promo; they just need to hear that you have new material out."

For that she was grateful and knew that she was so lucky and blessed. She worried that the break would change that. "Do you think they're going to forget me while I'm gone? I've talked a big game, but I'm kind of worried about it."

"No, they aren't going to forget you! They stalk your social media pages to see what you're doing with that hot hubby of yours. When you start posting more with him, they're going to be happy for you. There's always going to be people that are pissed, no matter what you do, but there are also people that are going to be extremely happy for you. Let's focus on those people."

Hannah quickly sent a text to Garrett thanking him for the flowers. She knew that he was awake if he knew she was in the top spot on iTunes, and that meant he'd either woken up early to check or he'd been up most of the night. Either way, she appreciated it more than she could say. "Have you decided what you're going to do?" she asked Shell, pushing her bangs back from her face.

Shell smirked. "Jared invited me on tour with him for some of the time. We're still in that kind of awkward stage—you know, where we don't know if we want to spend that much time together. But I also looked at some college courses online."

"Really?" Hannah squealed. "That's awesome, Shell! What are you thinking of studying."

"Believe it or not, business management with a focus on the music industry. Belmont's got a program. I feel like if you don't want to do this anymore, I could take a young up-and-coming artist and not let them get into the bullshit that we did. That's still a way off though, and I'll need to look at program requirements and all of that stuff. It's what I'm seriously thinking of doing."

Hannah hugged her friend. "I'm proud of you, and I'm so happy we've been able to get over this. I was worried when I told what I wanted to do, and the last thing I want to do is to ruin our friendship. I hope you understand that."

"I do. I had to get my head on straight, and you can thank Jared for that." Shell tightened her arms around her friend. They had been through so much together, and it was always going to be her first reaction to protect Hannah and to try to do what was best for her, but it was time now for Hannah to fly. It was time for her to find her own place, and that place would always be with her husband, just like Shell was beginning to learn that her place was with Jared.

"Enough of this mushy stuff. We have a few more songs to run through." Hannah wiped her eyes.

Before they could get the band rounded up, Hannah's phone rang, and she saw the face of Garrett on the screen. She excused herself to the hallway and answered. "Thanks so much for the flowers, they're gorgeous," she told him before he even said hello.

He laughed, the sound deep in her ear. "My pleasure, babe. I'm excited for you."

He sounded tired, very tired. "Have you been up all night?"

"Well, we got done recording around two a.m. our time, and when I got home, I knew iTunes would be updating from your side since it went live at midnight. I saw that it was already climbing, and I got excited, and then I couldn't stop myself from watching it like a hawk. I'm so proud of you. I think I'm more excited for you than for myself," he admitted.

"You should get some sleep. It's going to be a very long day for you if you don't," she told him, but the smile on her face was huge. To know that he'd taken the time to do that, that he'd been excited for her, caused her heart to warm. This was one of the reasons she loved him so much.

"I'm about to, but you know it's never the same without you here."

That melted her heart too. "Eight more weeks and then you're going to want me to go away."

"Never. I'm counting down those days. I can't wait to have you with me."

"Speaking of being with me." She twirled a strand of her hair around her finger. "I have a house I want you to look at in Brentwood. I sent you the link last night, but I didn't know if you had checked your email. The realtor said that he could show it to us separately or he could try to fit us in at the same time. I warn you though," she grinned, "it's expensive."

"How expensive are we talking, and do you like it from the pictures?"

"It's gorgeous from the pictures," she sighed. "It's in the millions of dollars range," she whispered.

"How many millions of dollars are we talking?" he asked, his voice holding an amused tone.

"Ohhh, around two-point-two-ish."

He laughed full on then. "Han, the house I live in here is a couple of million dollars too. Houses are more expensive here. It'll be good, we'll check it out."

"Okay, then," she sighed. "It's a lot of money."

"That we have together. This is the home that we're going to live in together in your hometown. We'll be fine," he soothed her nerves.

"Let me know what you think of it. I do love it, but if you're looking for something different, please let me know. I gotta go back to rehearsal."

"Okay, have fun, babe, and congrats. So much congrats."

"Thank you and please get some sleep." She blew a kiss into the phone, telling him that she loved him.

When they hung up, she went to her personal email account; snagged a picture from the photo shoot they'd done together and uploaded her favorite picture. Hashtagging it lucky girl, she smiled brightly. Her happiness was with him and she needed everyone in her life, including him, to know that.

Immediately, her phone went nuts, and she couldn't help but giggle at the comments from the women about Garrett. She loved it because she agreed with every single one of them.

The next eight weeks needed to get here and be gone.

Chapter Twelve

Hannah moved her head in a circle on her neck and then turned in the chair that she sat in, moaning as her back cracked loudly.

"Damn, did that feel good?" Shell asked, looking up from the bowl of cereal that she was eating.

The first few days of touring and sleeping on the bed in her tour bus always killed her back. "Yes, it's that freakin' bed. It's always so uncomfortable the first few days. How are numbers looking?" she asked Shell as she dug into the bowl of fruit that sat in front of her.

"Great, better than I think anyone expected. You're holding steady on the charts that are updated daily. I heard from the record company today, they are thinking you made top five on the all-genre Billboard, which would be your best showing ever. We'll find that out tomorrow. Every show so far has been sold out. Every single post you make on social media is blowing up, and the song has hit the top ten on the country chart. All in all, this has been an amazing release week. The record company is beyond happy." Shell looked at her friend. "But are you happy?"

"I'm excited that this has done everything we wanted to do, but now I'm getting nervous."

"What in the world for?"

"It's exceeding expectations. You and I both know that when expectations are exceeded, they want to extend tours, they want to add on dates and do more promotional appearances. What if they try to fight me exercising my clause?"

"That's not going to happen. You said yourself that your lawyer said it's iron-clad."

He had said that, and Hannah believed him with everything she had, but at the same time, she was waiting for the other shoe to drop. Things had never gone how she planned them before, and she was worried that this would be another one of those times. "I know, I just think I'm going to be on edge until the last show of this tour."

"It's nerves, Han. You've never asked them for anything like this before; you've never gone against anything before. You're nervous. It can't help that this has been the biggest opening week of your career and it's happening just as you're planning to take time off."

"How did that announcement go this week, by the way? I've kept myself away from anything having to do with it."

She and Shell had decided to be pro-active and let the fans know that she had decided to take some time off after the end of this small tour. That announcement had ended up coming the day after the album drop, and it hadn't affected sales, so she hoped for the best.

"Pretty supportive, but the same BS about you being pregnant and that's why you only want to tour for eight weeks."

"My gosh," she sighed. "What is with people's obsession with me being pregnant? I would love to actually get to enjoy my husband for a few months before we add a baby into the mix. If we add a baby into the mix this soon." It wasn't like she hadn't thought of it. She did every time they made love. There was a part of her that wanted it more than anything, but there was also another part of her that knew it was way too soon. They needed time on their own, and they needed time to figure out the dynamic of their married relationship before they added another stressor to it.

"Can you imagine how cute a baby Reaper would be?" Shell sipped her coffee. "I mean, my cold-ass heart is melting at the thought."

Hannah snickered, throwing a piece of fruit at her friend. "You do not have a cold heart, and to be honest I do imagine how cute a baby Reaper would be, but it's not the time for it yet."

"At least you know that fans will be all about it when it does happen, because according to tabloids you've already been pregnant five times."

"Whatever, I gotta get ready for this radio interview," she laughed, getting up from the booth in the bus. No matter how much she thought about it, she knew they weren't ready, but possibly it was something she could talk to him about during her time off.

"Your wifey is number three on the all-genre Billboard," Jared yelled to Garrett as he entered the recording studio later the next night.

"Oh shit, for real?" He ran over to the computer that Jared sat in front of, moving him out of the way to look for himself.

"For real. We've all been waiting for the chart to update, and it finally did."

Garrett thought it was amazing the way the guys had taken to her, almost as excited for the things going on with her as he was. There had been times in their relationship as a group that none of them had liked someone's girlfriend. It was important to him that they love his wife as much as they loved him. "That's amazing for her."

"It is." Jared smiled over at his friend. "Congrats, dude. You got a good one."

He knew that without a doubt, and he missed her something fierce. The two of them hadn't been able to get hooked up on FaceTime or Skype this entire week, and he missed seeing her face. He knew that she was incredibly busy, and with him being in the studio at night, it made it even more difficult than normal. "I know, I wish I could see her."

"Hopefully soon," Jared told him quietly. He, of all of them, knew what kind of schedule Hannah was keeping, and it was back-breaking for the time she'd allowed the record company. "When was the last time you talked to her?"

"A few days ago, but I haven't actually seen her in a week. This is the hard part," he told his friend, turning his wedding ring around on his finger. FaceTime or Skype at least allowed him to see her, and they hadn't even had time for that.

"If it wasn't hard, it wouldn't mean so much."

Jared had him there. It did mean a lot because it wasn't easy. He had never had to make such an effort to be with another woman. It wasn't his normal MO, and maybe that was why he loved her so much, why it meant so much to him that he had her. Dwelling too much on it would make him sad, and that's not where he wanted to go on this night. "When are we starting this damn session?" he asked, running his fingers through his hair. "I thought I was fuckin' late."

"You were," Brad looked at him pointedly, "but none of us wanted to say anything about it."

Garrett threw him a middle finger. "Where's our engineer?"

The door opened as he finished asking the question, and an intern peeked his head in. "Your engineer for the night has called in. He's got food poisoning. He said you could either come back tomorrow or you could try to do some stuff on your own, just don't fuck up his stuff."

When the door closed, the group looked at each other. "What are we gonna do?" Garrett asked, looking around the room. This didn't hold the appeal that it normally did. "It's been a while since we hit the neighborhood bar."

They all looked at Jared. "I will totally be the DD," he said, holding his hands up. "I've finally got my shit under control. Besides," he clapped his hand on Garrett's back. "I think my man here needs a night of debauchery."

The thought held a sort of promise. He did need to blow off some steam. He was sick of being stuck in California while Hannah was wherever she was for the night, and he missed her. He needed the feeling of peace that she gave him. Without that peace, Reaper had to come out, and to be honest, he wasn't sure how that was going to fly. "Promise me," he grabbed Jared's arm as the group made their way out of the studio. "Promise me that you won't let me get fuckin' stupid. It's been a while since I've done this, and I miss Hannah like I can't tell you."

Jared knew what that meant for his friend. He needed to blow off steam, and in the past, that had either meant he'd beat somebody with his fists until he was done or he'd find a groupie and fuck her until that peaceful feeling returned. "I promise."

The local bar was just as Garrett remembered—a dive with cheap drinks. He and the guys had a seat at the booth they had sat at since they'd started coming here when each of them had turned twenty-one. Their favorite waitress, Lisa, came over and already had a tray full of drinks and a bottle of Coke for Jared.

"Do you want me to keep them coming?" she asked.

Garrett tipped his head back, the shot burning as it went down his throat and into his belly. He chased it with a large drink of beer. "Fuck yes, keep it coming until they cut my ass off," he told her, holding up his credit card to her.

"Where's that cute wife of yours?" she asked, watching him with a critical eye. She'd known him for a long time.

"Somewhere on the other side of the United States

tonight."

"You better be careful," she warned him.

"I'm always careful," he assured her, flashing the smile at her that always got him what he wanted from other people.

"I'm serious, Garrett. This place is bursting with hot girls in tight-ass skirts. You be careful."

"Nobody is hotter than my wife." He waved her off.

She glanced at him, this time her eyes soft. "I know you miss her, but remember that I've been doing this a long time, and sometimes a warm body means much more than the memory of someone. You boys watch him. There's a group of women here that were hoping you guys would be in tonight."

Jared looked up at her. "He's not going to get out of line, I got it."

She seemed pacified by Jared's assurances and did what the group asked.

Over the course of the night, Garrett lost count of how many shots he'd taken. He texted Hannah at different intervals, telling her how much he missed her, the things he wanted to do to her when he had her alone. Checking his phone, he realized that she was on stage and she wouldn't be seeing her messages for hours. Maybe by that time, he would be sober again and he could have a normal conversation with her. Slamming back another shot, uncharacteristic tears filled his eyes. He didn't know how to deal with this, the feelings that came with her being gone. The emptiness he felt when she wasn't around. It had become increasingly worse, and he didn't know what to do. Never before had his life been so wrapped up in another person that he didn't know how to pull himself out of it. Sometimes he missed her so much it hurt to breathe.

"I gotta take a piss," Jared told him. "Don't get up from here, you're shitfaced as fuck."

Garret nodded, even though he wasn't sure he understood what Jared said to him. He looked across the table and saw that, at some point, Brad had invited Stacey and they were sitting close to each other, Brad whispering in her ear. "Dude, back off my sister," he said, but the words were slurred, and he wasn't sure that they could understand him because he could barely understand the words he'd meant to say.

Stacey rolled her eyes. "You're drunk, bro. It's fine."

Before he could answer, a dark-haired girl slid into the booth next to him, and for a moment, he thought it was Hannah. Then she turned so that she could see his face, and he knew without a doubt that this wasn't his wife.

"Take a picture with me?" she asked, her smile bright.

"Sure," he slurred, trying to hold his eyes open. Now all he wanted to do was go home and sleep it off. He turned so that he could be in the picture with her, and the girl settled herself right on his lap. That didn't sit well with him. "You need to move," he told her, putting his hands on her hips, trying to push her off.

"Just smile."

In the end, all he wanted to do was get it over with, so he did what she told him, barely able to hold his head up.

Chapter Thirteen

Hannah felt her stomach drop as she opened the link that had been sent to her. Did she really want to look at this? When she had called Garrett the night before, he had been ranting and raving about some woman who'd sat on his lap. He was drunk, so at first, she'd thought it was cute. He'd admitted to getting drunk because he'd missed her, that he'd needed some way to deal with the loneliness. That had torn her apart, had made her feel like crap because she knew how much she missed him. When he admitted things like that, it gutted her. She wished in those moments that she'd never told the record company that she would do this final tour. Seven more weeks, that's all they had to get through, but it felt like a million years.

"Have you seen it?" Shell asked as she came back to Hannah's bedroom and had a seat on the bed.

"No." She shook her head. "I'm not sure that I want to. Have you?"

"Yeah, and I've talked to Jared."

Jared had been the one person sober last night, so she was very interested to hear what he had to say.

"And?"

"He went to the bathroom for five minutes. He figures those girls were waiting for him to leave because he'd been sitting on the outside of the booth so that nobody could get to Garrett. As soon as he was gone, they must have moved in. Jared swears that Garrett could hardly hold his head up. He just kept talking about how much he missed you and how much he wanted to see you because it'd been so long since you'd even Skyped or FaceTimed."

That was true, and Hannah felt shame burn her face hot. They had become comfortable with just texting one another and the occasional phone call. Funny how quickly that had happened, that they'd become complacent. That was not what she had wanted at all. That wasn't how she wanted her marriage to work. Not how she wanted to make things easy when the staying together part became harder.

"Do you need to see this picture?" Shell asked her. "Will it change anything?"

"No, it won't change anything, but I do need to see it. I need to see and know that he couldn't keep his head up, that this person preyed on him because he was drunk. It would make me feel better. I know that's weak, but after Ashton, there are just certain things that I need to see with my own two eyes."

"Okay, but I'm warning you, I'm not even married to the guy and I want to kick her ass."

Hannah rolled her eyes. "Never in all my almost-twenty-five years have I wanted to kick someone's behind, I highly doubt I'm gonna start now." She opened the link and her eyes narrowed.

"I'm watching you, and it looks like you're irritated," Shell provided commentary.

"It's because I am," she whispered as she took a good look at the picture. She wouldn't say it out loud, but Hannah did want to kick this girl's ass.

"Irritated at him or the skank ho throwing herself at him."

"The skank ho," she breathed out. "He really couldn't hold his head up," she said, her voice thick with emotion.

Anyone who knew Garrett and looked at this picture could tell that he wasn't putting the moves on this girl. His lips were nowhere near her neck, his forehead rested on her shoulder. There was a series of pictures, and in the first one he looked irritated, while in the next one he was slumped over the table with his head in his hands.

"I can't believe the media is running with this," Shell told her. "If this was a woman, they'd all be talking about how he took advantage of her and blah, blah, blah."

Hannah had to agree. "I wonder if he's seen these yet."

"I would say he's in the process of sleeping off one of the worst hangovers of his life. This doesn't bother you at all?"

"I won't lie; I don't like seeing another woman perched on my husband's lap like that. I really don't like that his mouth is near her neck either, because that's my spot. I have to be realistic about this. I can't let the paparazzi win; they do things like this to get a rise out of us. I'm sure that's what this skank ho wanted too. While it doesn't feel good, and it makes me more than a little sick to my stomach, I'm not giving them what they want." Hannah's voice was thick with emotion. "What they want is to break us up, and that's not going to happen."

Shell couldn't believe the person talking to her was her best friend. At one time, this picture would have ruined her life and her self-esteem. She wouldn't have been able to concentrate on anything besides the picture. Then the questioning would start. Was this the first time he'd done something like this? Was he doing this behind her back? How many women had he had? In all honestly, Shell had prepared herself for the worst and was pleasantly surprised at what she was getting from her best friend. "I'm glad this isn't a huge deal."

"I know what you were probably expecting, but I am working very hard on not letting these jerks rule my life. I mean, look what I was going to do a few months ago—send myself back into that downward spiral of an eating disorder. I'm trying to be my own person and not let other people's issues affect me. I'm not gonna lie though, I would like to rip this chick's brown extensions out of her head."

Shell laughed. "Me too. I mean, he's married. Who asks a married man to pose like that, and when he's obviously that intoxicated? She gives women a bad name."

"I wish I had time to sit here and google her and see what all I could find out about her, but I have another flippin' radio interview," Hannah sighed.

"When they ask you about this, don't go off," Shell warned.

"I'll do my best." And that was all she could promise.

Garrett felt like his head was being pounded on by a herd of wild horses. Late afternoon sunlight streamed through the curtains of his bedroom, and he hugged the pillow tighter to his body. It was the one that Hannah always used and tended to smell like her for weeks after she was gone. Hannah, his eyes popped open as he heard more pounding. It wasn't just his head, someone was beating down his front door. Getting up on wobbly legs, he saw that he was still wearing his clothes from the night before. It was foggy, but he knew he had gone to the bar with the band. He was missing his wife, and everything after that was a blur.

"I'm coming," he whispered, not able to make his voice rise any louder at the pounding on the door. Finally he got there, swinging it open. Shit. It was his mom. What the fuck had he done?

"Garrett, you look like hell."

She didn't pull any punches as she swept by him, into his house.

"Come on in," he mumbled, putting his hand to his forehead. It hurt like a motherfucker, and he had the worst case of cottonmouth he'd ever had in his life.

"What's going on with you?" Marie did a once-over, curling her lip in disgust that he was still wearing his clothes from the night before. "I figured when you got married you would be done with all of this."

His brain wasn't firing on all cylinders, and he need-ed her to take a small step back in her judgment of him, but he didn't know how to say it. "I went out and got drunk last night because I miss my wife and we as a band had nothing better to do, that's it." He always thought he got his temper from his dad, until he pushed his mom to the breaking point. It wasn't often that it happened, but when it did, he was actually scared of her.

"No, son, that's not *it*." She spit the word out. "Do you even remember what happened last night?"

Suddenly he got a bad feeling. Had he done something that he didn't remember? He knew without a shadow of a doubt there had not been another woman in his bed, for that he could be thankful, but what had happened before he got home? "I went to the bar and started doing shots, after that it's kind of fuzzy," he admitted as he had a seat on his couch and tilted his head back against the cushions.

She watched him with what could only be described as an evil eye, pulling her smart phone from her purse and pressing a few buttons. When she had what she obviously wanted to show him, she whipped it around in his face. "This looks like a hell of a lot more than doing shots."

"The fuck?" he asked as he saw the picture of him with a brown-headed girl. She was sitting in his lap, and he had his head on her neck. From the angle, it looked almost like he was trying to kiss her, but when he took a good look; he saw that his forehead rested against her shoulder. He probably hadn't been able to keep his head up at that point.

"That's my question. Why would you go and do something like this?"

"I don't even remember it. Jared promised me that he wouldn't let me do anything stupid." Where had Jared been?

"I already talked to him. He took a five-minute bathroom break, and when he came back, this was going down," she told him. "But Jared isn't responsible for you making good decisions. Have you heard from Hannah? I'm sure she's seen this."

Fuck. His wife. "I woke up to you pounding on my fucking front door, Mom. No, I haven't talked to my wife yet." Fear took hold around his stomach. They were at a good place. What if this caused a setback?

"I think you need to call her."

This was all too much. He was hung over; he needed water, aspirin, and a shower to be able to think straight. He was going to lose his shit, and he didn't want to do that with his mom. "I think you need to get the fuck out of my house. She's my wife; I'll do what I need to do."

"Don't talk to me like that, son." She emphasized the word son.

He sighed. "I know you mean well, but I will take care of this in my own way. I love you, but I really need you to leave."

Marie hesitated, then walked over to where he sat, pulling him up for a hug. "No matter how old you get, I want to fix things for you, and I'm going to give you some unsolicited advice right now. Call your wife, apologize, tell her you love her, and for the love of God, take a shower. You stink to high heaven."

He smirked, a small chuckle coming from his throat. "Will do, Mom. Thanks for coming to check on me."

"It's what we do. Love you," she told him as she let herself out of the house.

Suddenly feeling tired again, Garrett fell back against the couch cushions. What the fuck was he going to do now? How did he explain this to Hannah? He couldn't even make his finger move over the button that he knew would connect them on his phone. The dilemma was answered for him when the phone vibrated in his hand and he saw the picture of the person that he most wanted to see. He wasn't sure how he would be received when he answered, but he knew he had to answer. Swiping his thumb across the screen, Hannah's picture disappeared and the call engaged.

"Hey, beautiful," he answered, hoping with everything he had that a little sweet talk was what she needed to forgive him.

Chapter Fourteen

Judging from the way Garrett's voice sounded, he was not having a good day. "How are you?" she asked, carefully.

He cleared his throat twice and then cursed. "Fuck this, answer my FaceTime, I need to see you."

The call disengaged, and then she got his FaceTime request. Accepting it, she was surprised at the way he looked. Her mouth hung open and she whistled.

"I know, I look like hell."

"Garrett, babe, what did you do to yourself last night?" she questioned, her eyes taking in his appearance. He looked awful.

"Something very stupid if the tabloids are to be believed."

Hannah could see the guilt on his face, could almost physically feel it through the phone. "Did you wake up by yourself this morning?" she whispered.

"Fuck, Han, I was drunk, but I wasn't that drunk."

"Are you sure? Because from what I saw, you could barely hold your head up."

The hurt was there in her eyes as he watched but so

was anger. She was mad. "I know it looked bad."

"It did, almost as bad as the pictures with me and Bryson." She took a deep breath, trying to calm herself down. "What we have to remember is that not everybody is happy about our marriage. There are some people that want it gone or want to see us struggle. We have got to stop putting ourselves in situations like this."

She was right. He had been a dumbass to think he could go out in public and drink his loneliness away. He should have done it in the comfort of his home with his friends. They were no longer the locally known band that everybody wanted to buy a drink. They were now internationally known, and some people chomped at the bit to wait for them to fail. He couldn't put himself in that situation again, not when it threatened what he had with her.

"I'm so fuckin' sorry."

Hannah smiled brightly at him, and that was almost his undoing. "I can tell by looking at the picture that you were not into it. I'm not mad at you, honest. I'm mad at her, whoever she is. When did we, as women, stop having respect for ourselves?"

"God, I love you," he chuckled. "We're okay?"

"We are fine. I'm confident in what we have here. The two of us need to remember who we are. Even though we see ourselves as normal, we have to remember that not everybody else sees us that way. Let's promise now that we stop putting ourselves in these situations."

Somehow the roles had reversed. "As funny as this sounds, I'm proud of you for being the one to lift me up this time."

She laughed loudly. "It is kind of weird, huh? I guess it's what we do when we love each other." Her eyes shone brightly with the laughter.

"I can't wait to see you," he told her softly. He wanted so much to reach through the screen of the phone and push her hair back from her face.

"I can't either. Have you taken a look at your schedule?"

"I have," he nodded. "I think I can make it out for a day next week. I know you can't do anything, they've fuckin' booked you solid."

Hannah groaned and frowned. "Shell and I received the last of my dates yesterday. In this entire eight-week stretch, I have a total of five days off. Can you believe that?"

"They want to be sure and cash in." He rolled his eyes. "Seven more weeks, and I can see you next week. We got this."

She hoped he was right. It was hard to feel completely confident when everything was working against you. "What day do you think you can make it out next week? One of my days off is next week. Maybe we can meet in Nashville and tour that house?"

"You are so excited about that damn house." He shook his head.

"I am!"

"Okay," he relented. "Send me when and where, and I'll be there with bells on."

"Sounds good." She clapped her hands. "I gotta go for now, I have a radio interview. Be sure and take a shower, cause you look like you stink."

"Love you too."

She blew a kiss at him. "I do love you, that's why I'm being honest. I'll see you in a few days?"

"See ya."

He disconnected, glad that he had been able to call her and get it worked out. The countdown was now on for next week.

Hannah stood in Nashville International Airport waiting for Garrett to walk through the baggage claim area. He'd texted her five minutes ago that he'd landed.

"I hate to bother you, Harmony, but do you think I could have an autograph?"

That soft voice interrupted Hannah's stalking of the entrance, and she glanced around, seeing a girl who was probably in her early teens. An older woman came to a stop behind the girl.

"I'm so sorry, I told her that you were busy, but she got away from me," the woman told her, her breath coming quickly.

"It's okay," Hannah told them, smiling as best she could. "Do you have anything for me to sign?"

Sometimes it was hard to be polite, especially when her heart was in her throat, waiting for the other half of her soul to meet her. It had been a long week, and all she wanted to do was let Garrett wrap his arms around her and tell her that everything was going to be okay. Sometimes, though, duty called. She watched as the girl reached into her messenger bag and pulled out a Sharpie, along with a notebook.

"Can you sign here?" she asked, indicating the first

page.

"Am I the first one?" Hannah asked, noticing that the notebook looked brand new. That was kind of exciting.

The girl nodded. "We're here on vacation for the week, and I was hoping to run into some people to get autographs from. You were the number-one person I wanted, I can't tell you how excited I am about this."

"Aww, thank you," she told the girl. Her excitement and nervousness over seeing Garrett abated a little. It was this girl's dream to meet her. "What's your name?"

"Madison."

Hannah started signing and decided to keep the conversation going. Garrett wasn't anywhere to be seen yet, anyway. "Have you wanted to come to Nashville for long?"

"Yes." The girl nodded, not offering anymore.

Glancing up at the mother, Hannah noticed tears in her eyes. The way the girl had said yes made her think there was more to the story.

"It's what kept her going," the mother whispered.

Hannah didn't have to ask. "I just went into remission from cancer," the girl told her. "This is my dream come true."

"Wow." Hannah breathed to keep the tears from coming to her eyes as well. She hated that people had to go through these things, especially children. "Do you wanna take a picture?" she asked, as she finished signing the notebook.

Madison nodded. "Can I take one with him too?" She pointed behind Hannah.

Hannah glanced behind her, noticing that her husband now stood patiently waiting. "I don't know," she winked at him. "You'll have to ask Reaper yourself."

He caught Hannah around the neck, pulling her flush to him. Her back to his front. "She likes to try and make me blush. What's your name, sweetheart?" he asked as he let go of Hannah and motioned for the notebook.

"Where are you and Madison staying?" she asked the mother while Garrett kept Madison entertained.

She rattled off the name of a hotel that Hannah knew wasn't in the best part of town. "You don't want to stay there, trust me." Putting her hand on the older woman's shoulder, she pulled out her cell phone and spent a couple of minutes texting while they continued to make small talk. "Okay, you're set up. I want you and Madison to have a great time. There's a car waiting outside for you, it will take you to the hotel that I've booked for you for the week, this car will also be at your disposal for your trip here. Have a great time, and if you need anything, don't hesitate to call my assistant, Shell." She wrote Shell's number on the back of a card and handed it to the woman.

If someone had asked her, she would never be able to tell them why she felt the need to do this. She'd never done anything like this before, but there was something about this girl and this woman that made her want to help. She didn't have to do it in front of a group of people, and she didn't even want a thank you. The tears in the older woman's eyes was enough.

Garrett put his arm around Hannah again as he and Madison came to stand closer to them. He reached out and shook the mother's hand. "It's a pleasure to be able to be number two in her book. I hope you have a great time in Nashville; I'm still learning about it myself, but what I've seen so far, I love."

His words seem to put the other woman at ease—it gave her time to get control of her emotions. They took two more pictures, and then Hannah hugged the mother. "Have a great time."

She and Garrett quickly made their way out of the hustle and bustle of the airport to her Land Rover that her mom had dropped off at the airport for her earlier in the day. Once there, he grabbed her up in a hug, kissing her softly on the lips before opening the passenger side door for her.

"I'm excited that we both got here around the same time." She grabbed his hand as he backed out of the parking spot.

"Me too, but I'm getting to where I fucking hate airports."

She frowned at his choice of words. "We got out of there just in time; we have to meet the realtor in an hour, and it's going to take us a little while to get across town."

He grinned over at her. "Have you seen it yet?"

"No, I've been waiting on you." She bounced in her seat.

Hannah wasn't sure why she was so excited, she just knew that this felt like another part of the progression of their lives as a married couple. This was the type of thing she saw them doing when they got married, not flying red-eyes at all hours trying to see each other for a few minutes here and there. She had to keep reminding herself that it would all work out in the end. She had to believe that.

Chapter Fifteen

When they pulled up to the address that Hannah had put into the GPS, Garrett whistled. "This is awesome."

"I know." She clapped her hands together with excitement. In person, she could see that the pictures on the internet didn't do the house justice. She had loved the gray exterior in the pictures she had seen, but in reality, it blended in so well with the surroundings that it looked as if it had been carved out of the landscape. When she got out of the SUV, she glanced around the property and noticed that she also liked the land it sat on. While the house was in a subdivision, it still had a little over two acres worth of land. The house sat in what she thought to be the middle of those two acres.

"Hannah?" A man in a suit approached her.

She smiled and stuck out a hand when she noticed it was the real estate agent that she had seen a picture of on the website. "Hi. Jacob, right?"

"Yes, it's a pleasure to meet you."

"Same here. This is my husband, Garrett." She introduced the two of them and waited while they shook hands, and then Jacob rolled up his shirt sleeve to show Garrett a Black Friday tattoo he had.

"If I wasn't a rocker, I would be the same way, dude," Garrett laughed. "All buttoned up with my tats a secret, so I could make it in the corporate world."

"Okay, so Hannah, I've told you everything I know about the house, I toured it the other day and it's spectacular. Do either of you have any questions for me?" he asked as they made their way to the front door.

"Can we, for the love of God, go in?" she asked, impatient.

He laughed, used to people being excited to tour the house that they wanted to make their own. "We sure can." He disengaged the lock that was on the front door, and then stepped in, turning off the alarm system before he motioned them in.

Garrett grabbed her hand, pulling her in behind him. "So this place is already equipped with security?"

"It is," Jacob answered. "The person who owns the house now is a well-known producer, and at one point had people dropping off CDs and drives with songs on them all the time. Word has it that someone got a little over-zealous and actually got into the house one night. He upped the security after that. Should you decide to make an offer on this house, the security is top-notch, and we can go into that at the end if you want."

Garrett nodded, feeling better about the situation. He wanted Hannah to be safe when he wasn't around. Finally, he allowed himself to take a look at his surroundings. There was a definite cultural difference from California houses to houses in Tennessee.

"While this is modern," Jacob was saying, "you'll still

see a lot of hallmarks of southern homes, which Hannah will probably get a whole lot more than you."

"I love these hardwood floors." Hannah's eyes were already bright, and they were only in the foyer.

"It's not hardwood through-out, but for the most part it is. There is a mother-in-law suite, which you could see to the left of the house when you pulled up, that's connected by a walk-way. It's being used right now as an office, and it has carpet, as well as the movie room. There's tile in the dining room too, it's got a nice mixture, I think."

"There's a movie room?" Garrett asked, eyebrows high and a bright smile on his face at the sound of that.

"Yes, there is," he confirmed, consulting the printed-out folder he had in front of him.

"I sent you the link," Hannah gently scolded him. "Didn't you take a look at it?"

"Kind of." He shrugged. "I didn't really need to. If you're excited, I'm excited." He slung an arm around her shoulders.

"I guess that's sweet, but I wanted you to know what you would be coming to look at."

"I do like it," he assured her. "The pictures that I did see didn't do this place justice."

They made their way further in, both admiring the lighting coming from the large windows and the big rooms.

"It's going to take a lot of furniture to fill this place up," she laughed as she held onto Garrett's arm.

"Or a lot of kids," Jacob joked. "It's got four bed-rooms."

They glanced at one another; neither of them had

broached that topic yet. "Someday," Hannah answered, vaguely.

They passed through a kitchen that would have made any chef jealous, through a dining room, and out onto a back wrap-around porch.

"The only thing that does suck is that you can't hear the ocean," Garrett told her, wrinkling his nose.

"Sacrifices." She winked. "We both have to make them."

"The living room isn't huge, but it's got a really nice stone fireplace," Jacob said as he led them back into the house.

"Does it ever get cold enough here to use that?" Garrett asked.

Jacob and Hannah glanced at one another, both wearing looks of amusement. "He only has to wait until the first snow shuts down the city," Jacob laughed.

"Snow? You don't get a lot here do you?" Garret asked.

"Doesn't take a lot," Hannah told him dryly. "Half an inch, a few flakes, whatever—it shuts down the city.

"Can you please do me a favor if you buy this house? The first time he's here when winter weather madness strikes, let me know how he handles it," Jacob laughed.

She really liked the realtor and hoped that Garrett would agree with her in putting an offer on the house. "Will do. It will be one of the most interesting days of my life, I can tell you that!"

The bathroom was more extravagant than she had been able to see in the pictures too. It held a makeup vanity and a huge walk-in closet. Garrett, in turn, loved the theater room and was already making plans on what he would change. When they made their way over to the mother-in-law suite, both of them were talking about making it their own studio. When the tour was over, they stood in the driveway with Jacob.

"Thank you for taking us through it today," Garrett told him, holding out his hand for him to shake.

"My pleasure, and to let you both know, there is some wiggle room in the price. If you want to make an offer, please contact the office. This is a very motivated seller who wants people who will enjoy this house, and the two of you have had smiles on your faces since you got here."

"We'll be in touch, as soon as possible," Hannah told him.

When they got into the Land Rover, they looked at each other and at the same time said, "We're making an offer."

"How long do you think we'll have to wait to hear back on our offer?" Hannah asked later on that night as the two of them lay on her couch.

Shell had decided not to fly in for the day with her, so they were alone, and enjoying the peace and quiet.

"I would say at least a few days. I know you're excited, babe, but try not to get your hopes up until we hear back. There may have been another couple after us that he showed it to."

"I hope not." She pulled her bottom lip between her teeth. "I love that house, and I feel at home there. You know when you walk in somewhere and you instantly know that's where you should live? I got that vibe there."

"I did too," he admitted. "That's a lot of bedrooms though," he laughed.

"I'm sure at some point we'll talk about having children, and we'll need that space," she mentioned, quietly. It wasn't necessarily something that she had given much thought to before, but since they had brought up the topic, she felt like she needed to throw that out there.

"With your break coming up, it might be the perfect time to talk about it." His green eyes bore into hers.

Hannah's stomach did a tumble when she thought about having his child. That was something she had always thought was so far off, but obviously if he had mentioned it, he was thinking about it. "Do you think it's too early to be talking about it?"

"No, do you?" He pushed her hair back from her neck, burying his face there.

"I feel like we should have a little time to ourselves first."

"I'm not saying let's get busy the first night that you get off tour. I'm saying sometime in the next year and a half," he chuckled.

That sounded better, something that she could deal with easier. Everything was so fast in their relationship that she was half afraid that it would be over as quickly as it had begun.

"You tensed, what's wrong?"

"There are moments," she sighed, "when I wonder if we've done this way too fast. I wonder if we're setting ourselves up for an epic crash and burn. I know that I shouldn't think that—no one wants to think that about any relationship they're in—but those thoughts sneak up on me sometime."

He swallowed hard against the lump that rose in his throat every time she questioned what they had. "You can't let that insecurity get into your head, babe. Things aren't easy for us, they never will be. Even if you decide to not go back to performing, I still will be. This is our reality, and we have to find a way to be okay with it. I think spending more time together will help us become more comfortable in what we have, but you can't let that shit get to you."

"I know." She ran her hand through her hair. "I don't know why I do this to myself."

"You're stressed, you're tired, and you want to be a normal person for a while, I get it, okay. You don't have to ever worry that I'm going to not get it, because I do. I have these moments too, I just don't voice them. I feel like if I voice them, then I give them power to make me question things, and that is never what I want to do with our relationship. We are different, though. You do what you need to do. I'm going to be right here with you every time you feel overwhelmed or have doubts."

"Because together we are stronger than we ever were apart." She clasped their hands, loving the feel of the strength he gave her with such a simple touch.

"Exactly. Nobody can break this as long as we don't let go." He tightened the grip. "And I'm damn strong, not to mention stubborn as fuck. We're going to figure this out."

"I know." She burrowed closer to him, glad to feel the warmth of his body, the beat of his heart. They would figure it out, she knew that, but the getting there was going to be a bumpy ride.

Chapter Sixteen

Hannah was tired, beyond tired. Glancing at the clock, she saw that it read five a.m., but she couldn't sleep. Her mind was traveling at a hundred miles a minute, and she could not get it to be quiet. She had even done the calming exercises that she'd found online. There were so many things she wanted to do, so many things that needed to get done, and she couldn't turn it off. Her and Garrett's offer on the house had been accepted, and they were looking to close on it in the next two weeks. Decorating ideas and Pinterest were now her best friends. Pulling her phone off her bedside table, she opened the calendar and counted. Five more weeks on this tour, she could do it. If she said it enough times, then it would be true. But God, she was so tired. Hannah quickly calculated the time in California and decided that Garrett was probably still awake. Pressing the button to FaceTime, she held her breath, waiting to see if he would answer.

"Babe, what the fuck are you doing awake? Not that I'm not excited to see you, but it's late."

His face came onto the screen, and she wanted to

cry. "I can't sleep," she told him, swallowing hard against the lump that had appeared in her throat.

"Are you okay?" he asked, his green eyes softening as he took in her face. There were huge dark circles under her eyes, and she looked on the verge of tears.

"I really need a hug." She smiled, but it was shaky.

He closed his eyes against the image on his phone. "God, Hannah, you're fucking killing me. I can't stand to see that look on your face and know that there's nothing that I can do about it."

Melancholy had taken over as soon as she'd seen him, the want to be near him and the need to have him with her. "I don't know that I can handle five more weeks," her voice broke against the words she said.

"Tell me what's wrong, and I swear to you, I will do whatever I can to fix it. It's killing me to see you like this and know that I'm across the country."

She blew out a deep breath, letting the tears fall from her eyes. "I'm tired, I'm PMS-ing, and I'm sad," she bit out, her voice thin. "I need a chocolate bar and some Midol, stat. A good cry would help too."

This was so out of his element. He'd never dealt with a hormonal wife before, and he wondered why that was. "You're never this hormonal, are you sure this is all that's wrong?"

She propped herself up on the pillows and ran her hand through her hair. "I'm so tired and I miss you. My brain will not shut the fuck up, and I want your arms around me in the worst way."

His eyebrows were to his hair line as he heard the f-word fly from her mouth. "I'm shocked at the word that came out of your mouth right now."

"I know, I am too." She blew out a frustrated breath. "I want to be normal. I'm sick of the separation and everything that goes with it. I feel like I'm a pawn in someone's game. They want me to do an eight-week tour in order for me to get time off, and then they pack everything they possibly can into that those eight weeks. It's so frustrating."

He glanced at the calendar. "Are you sure this isn't because you have that new song coming out tomorrow. The one you wanted me to duet on and the record companies both said no? Are you feeling pissed about it?"

"A little," she admitted. "I mean, it's like they don't want us to be married. I get these stupid messages from the record company—be careful how much of your husband you put on social media, we don't want to offend the fans. What the crap? I am an almost twenty-five-year-old newlywed. I am sick to death of being told what I can and what I cannot do. I'm ready to go AWOL on this tour." She pulled her bottom lip between her teeth. "I am done with it, Garrett. I need a break."

"Five weeks is not that long in the grand scheme of things," he played devil's advocate. The reality of it was, he heard the same things too. Probably not to the extent that she did, but every once in a while, there were grumblings about a rocker being married to a country star, and he had to defend his decisions. It was stupid because they were human beings like everyone else on the planet. No one batted an eye when normal people got married. "Your day off is tomorrow, right?"

"Yeah." But she wasn't excited about it. It was just another day that she was away from him.

"Maybe you need to do something for yourself, go shopping or see a movie. Spend the day in bed watching chick flicks until you're non-hormonal," he suggested.

Nothing sounded good to her except spending the day watching chick flicks wrapped up in his arms. No one seemed to understand. "Maybe," her voice was non-committal, and she fought not to roll her eyes. He was supposed to understand.

"I can't change our circumstances, Han. I see the disappointment in your face."

"I know you can't." She was beginning to get angry, and that was the last thing she wanted to do. "Whatever's meant to happen will happen, right?" Her tone was flippant and she smacked her hand against the mattress.

"Don't get pissed at me, don't you think I miss you too?"

Faced with that question and as moody as she was, she was feeling mean. "No, I don't. I think you have a good time in the studio with your friends every night and then go home and play video games or work out. Plus you have Havock there to keep you company, what do you need me for?"

That wasn't fair. That was how he wound down. How he dealt with the loneliness of the house without her being there. "You're being a dumbass right now." His temper was starting to get hot.

"What?" she breathed.

Her brown eyes flashed with anger as he stared into the phone, but she wasn't the only one who could get angry. "I said you're being a dumbass right now."

"I can't believe you would say those words to me."

"Well they're damn well true, and I'm fucking pissed.

Don't you dare sit there and tell me that I don't miss you, that I don't have the same sense of loneliness that you do. I'm willing to cut you a break 'cause you're on the rag, but kiss my ass."

That was crude. "Really?" she questioned him. "You're really gonna talk to me like that."

"Baby doll, you started it, so you damn well better be able to take it."

She opened her mouth, ready to lay into him, when he cut her off.

"You sit here, in this house every night, every motherfucking night, and tell me that I'm not lonely. I re-live everything we did here. When I go to bed, your pillow still smells like you. I barely get any sleep because all I do is think about what we did there. I can't look out at my balcony without imagining you spread over that table; gets me hard every time. You aren't here, so I do what I gotta do. Downstairs? Can't sit on the couch, we laid there watching movies for days, those motherfucking pillows smell like you too. Kitchen? We cooked breakfast there, and I can't sit at the fucking table without thinking of you sitting across from me. Beach? We walked there for hours playing with Havock. Bathroom? We had the biggest heart-to-heart of all there. Not to mention Havock. My fucking dog looks for you everywhere and sleeps on a shirt you left. I tried to pick it up off the floor to wash it for you, he nipped at me. Tried to bite me. There is absolutely no fucking way you can sit here and tell me that I don't understand what you're going through. I am surrounded by memories that you and I made, and I can't get away from them."

The tears that Hannah had tried to hold at bay

spilled over her eyes and down her cheeks. She wanted to say so many things, but he had gotten on a roll and she couldn't interrupt.

"You are a crazy fucking woman if you don't think I'm not affected by you not being here, and to be perfectly honest with you, that pisses me off, hurts my feelings, and pisses me off."

"You already said that pisses you off," she whispered, taken back by the way his green eyes flashed at her.

"Don't you dare be a smartass with me. I'm mad now, furious, that you discounted my feelings, and you think you have the monopoly on being sad, lonely, and depressed. I may not have the lady parts to have PMS, but I guarantee you my mood now matches yours. Congratulations, love of my life."

She couldn't get a word in edgewise.

He growled in frustration. "This is not the type of shit I need from you. What I need is for you to be the understanding wife who can't wait to see me. Not give me a fucking guilt trip because we can't be in the same time zone."

"I can't wait to see you," she whispered.

Reaper was on, and Garrett had taken a backseat. "You're a spoiled little brat if you want to act like you're the only one hurting here, and I don't want to hear about it anymore. Have a good fucking day, sweetheart." He disconnected the call.

She was left holding the phone, her mouth hanging open in shock. There was a knock at the door and Shell opened it without hesitation.

"Was that Garrett I heard yelling in here?"

For a moment Hannah didn't say anything, still looking at the phone, thinking she would see him try to reconnect their FaceTime. When it became apparent that he wasn't going to do that, she lowered the phone to her lap and looked at her friend. "Yeah," she nodded before bursting into tears.

"Did you two have a fight?" Shell asked, climbing onto the bed next to her and hugging her close.

"I'm not sure what that was." She shook her head. Once she had her emotions somewhat under control, she explained to Shell what had happened.

"I can't believe I'm defending him, but you're both very stressed, and sometimes we snap at the people we love the most. You know he's got a hair trigger sometimes. Did you deserve it? Probably not, but we both knew it was coming."

"No." Hannah shook her head. "I didn't know it was coming."

"Well, I did. Jared told me that Garrett's been an ass to be around the past few days. He misses you, and he's having a hard time dealing with it."

"This is stupid." Hannah ran her hand through her hair. "Why can't we be normal? Why do we have to go through this separation, and then why in the world do we have to get annoyed with and yell at each other?"

"You're newlyweds, Han. Most newlyweds fight just to make up. I have a feeling that's what you two are doing. The only bad thing for you? He's too far away for makeup sex," she giggled.

Hannah groaned. "Five more weeks. I can handle five more weeks, right?"

In her own head, Shell wondered if she could handle

five more weeks with her friend. Hannah and Garrett were going to drive her insane before this was all over. Instead of voicing that, she nodded her head. "You got this."

"I got this," Hannah repeated, but knew she didn't have it at all.

Chapter Seventeen

"**F**ucking crazy-ass females." Garrett slammed his phone against his thigh.

"What's wrong?" Jared asked. They were still in the studio, trying to finish up the song they were working on. Everyone else had left for the night. Out of the entire group, he and Jared were the most dedicated and they all knew it.

"Did you catch the end of that?"

"Kind of, I tried to give you your privacy, but I couldn't help but hear. You did have her on FaceTime."

"Was I harsh?" he asked, needing to feel justification for his feelings, and if anyone could give it to him straight, it was Jared.

"You're always harsh when you care. That's the thing, you have no filter, and sometimes that's hard for people to take. Especially when people aren't used to that side of you. Even though she's your wife, she's not used to that side of you. With her, you still have to watch yourself."

There were some things he couldn't let go, and he knew that about himself. Her seriously questioning whether he missed her or not was one of those things. It wasn't like they were in a contest over who missed each other the most, but his feelings still mattered. "I'm sick of her acting like I don't give a shit."

"Do you wonder if that's a mechanism? Ever?" Jared asked quietly.

"No, and I really don't give a fuck. If she can't figure out that I give a shit after everything we've been through, then what am I fighting so hard for?"

"I want you to hear me out."

Garrett wasn't sure that he wanted to do that. Jared was the king at making excuses, and Garrett was more than sure he could do it for Hannah too. What he wanted to do more than anything in this moment was to shut down and not give a fuck. It didn't hurt when he didn't give a fuck.

"I'm going to take you not saying anything as it being okay for me to speak. As someone who has a lot of the same personality traits as she does, I can tell you that acting like someone doesn't care is an easy way of making it not hurt so much. If you believe that someone doesn't care, then it doesn't mean anything. Remember all those times I told you that I didn't have your perfect life, so there was no way you'd understand what I was going through? It made it easier to pretend you didn't understand."

"But I'm so damn sick of proving I do understand, that I do miss her."

"And I'm sure she's sick of hearing you lose your cool. These are two things that the two of you are going to have to work on. You're newlyweds who got married months after meeting each other. These are personality quirks. Quirks that you will learn to work around. I'm not saying you should be the one to apologize, but I'm saying that the two of you need to come to some sort of understanding," Jared offered, taking a drink from the bottle of water he now carried with him everywhere.

"It's hard to do that when we have no time to spend together."

"And there lies the problem." Jared looked at him pointedly. "She's killing herself to give you two this time."

"It's not my fault," Garrett cut him off.

"No, it's not, but at the same time, you need to think of how tired, stressed, and sick of running around she is. They are demanding a lot from her, and so are you."

Garrett ran his hands through his hair, pulling on the ends of it. "I don't know what to do, I'm not the one who's going to apologize all the fucking time, I'm not."

"It's not about the apology, it's about the under-standing."

Jared got up and walked out of the studio. He had done what he thought was right, and that was all he could do.

It was going on forty-eight hours since she and Garrett had spoken to one another. As much as she hated to admit it, she had spent her day off in her bed, watching chick flicks and drinking Starbucks. That pissed her off more than she cared to tell anyone, but he had been right, it was exactly what she needed. Now she wasn't sure how to approach him, to tell him that she was sorry and she shouldn't have flown off the handle when they talked. She should have been as supportive to him as he was to her, and her emotions and hormones had gotten the better of her. It wasn't very often in her world that she had to make amends. She glanced at her cell phone; she had two hours before she had to start getting ready for her show. Grabbing her laptop, she pulled it over to where she sat.

"What's going on?" Shell asked as she walked into the room and had a seat in the chair that sat next to Hannah.

"Looking for something to give to Garrett. An 'I'm sorry' gift."

"What do you get for the guy who has everything?" Shell asked, as she scrolled through texts on her phone.

"I know, right? He has anything he could ever want, and I'm not sure what I could get him that he doesn't have, but I've got to find something." She started searching random things and blew her hair out of her face as she came up with absolutely nothing.

"What do you love about him?" Shell asked.

"Everything," Hannah answered without hesitation.

"No, like, make a list. That way we can see what we can buy."

Hannah started marking off things. "I love his tattoos, his good heart, the fact that he has to wear prescription glasses and it's all a part of his *him*. I love all of that."

Shell snapped her fingers, an idea popping into her head. "What about earrings? He's worn the same pair since we met him."

"That's an awesome idea." Hannah sat up straighter

in her chair. "The only problem is his ears aren't normal. They're gauged or something like that."

"Let me text Jared," she said, as she grabbed her phone and began typing a message to her boyfriend.

"Tell him not to say anything," Hannah warned.

"Trust me; our secret is safe with Jared."

An hour later, she had picked out a pair, and thanks to some quick talking from Shell, who was much more assertive, the earrings were being delivered that afternoon to the studio, where Jared assured her they would be.

"Thanks for helping me," Hannah told her as she sat down in her makeup chair and started applying products. A lot of singers had professionals that helped, but she preferred to do her own makeup, always had.

"You're welcome. I know you've been stressed and tired and you miss him. If I can make anything easier for you, then I want to. Sometimes it's hard for me to know what to do to make things easier for you. I try, but it can be difficult."

"It's because I don't want people to think I can't do things on my own. When I met Garrett and he started pointing out how much you do for me, it made me realize how much I had come to count on you doing everything for me. That wasn't fair for you. It wasn't even fair to me, because then it was like I couldn't be an adult. Now I'm struggling with asking for help. Am I going to become that dependent person again? I'm overwhelmed, but I can't tell if it's because I have a ton going on or if it's because I'm a brat like Garrett said," she laughed. The first time she'd laughed in days.

"He wasn't wrong about anything he said; I can be

honest enough with you to tell you that. At the same time, all of us can be the same way. All of us have periods of time when we're just flat-out bitches, and he caught you at a bad time; apparently you caught him at a bad time too. At some point, one of you is going to have to call the other one," Shell told her. "I can't believe it's been two days."

"I think it's the principle that neither one of us wants to give in."

"Someone is going to have to."

Hannah made a non-committal sound as she finished her makeup and called for hair.

Thirty minutes before show time was always a nervous time for Hannah. She would sit backstage and go through the set list, make sure her voice was good to go, and drink a coffee or energy drink to make sure she was ready. On this night, she couldn't think of any of that, all she could think of was the fact that she and Garrett still hadn't spoken to each other. It wasn't that she hadn't wanted to call him, she didn't mind being the one to make the move, but she was afraid that he wouldn't pick up the phone, and she wasn't sure that her confidence could take that yet.

The phone that sat in her hand buzzed, and she unlocked the screen so she could see why. There was a notification from Instagram. It was from Garrett. It was a picture of him wearing the earrings that she and Shell had picked out.

"My amazingly gorgeous and generous wife sent

these to me today. Love them @HarmonyStewart – love you and see you soon."

The smile she wore was bright, it wasn't a phone call from him, but he had mentioned her, and he had obviously loved the gift, judging by the smile on his face. It was a step in the right direction, and she had to wonder what the "see you soon" meant. A knock on the door caused her to look up.

"You have a delivery from California," Shell told her, carrying a bag and a basket into the room.

Her heart sank slightly. There was a part of her that had hoped it would be Garrett standing there. "Thanks." She got up and walked over to where Shell stood. Opening it, she glanced inside and burst out laughing.

"What is it?"

She pulled out the objects: a package of chocolate bars, a big box of Midol, and a bundle of chick flick DVDs. Along with everything was a note. "This is what I should have done instead of flying off the handle. I will see you soon, I love you, and I'm not sorry for what I said because I meant it, but I'm sorry for the tone, and I'm sorry for taking my bad day out on you."

His message pretty much mirrored the one that she had sent him with the earrings. She could breathe again, she realized as she took a deep breath. Pulling her phone out, she glanced at her calendar. The argument had pushed them to the four-week mark. Four more weeks and then she would be done. Knowing that they could overcome their arguments, even if it did take them a few days, gave her the courage to know that they could handle this. Twenty-eight days, less than a month. They had this. They absolutely had this.

"Harmony, we need you in a few minutes," one of the stage hands told her.

"Be right there." She rushed back to her dressing area and took off the shirt she originally was going to wear. She shuffled through the clothes that hung there. Once she found the "Reaper's Girl" shirt that he'd given her the first day they'd hung out with one another, she put it on, along with a tank top. Quickly she took a selfie and posted it, along with the caption. "Always have been and always will be."

They were going to be fine. She had to keep reminding herself of that.

Chapter Eighteen

As she came off-stage, her phone was ringing. Garrett's face stared back at her, and she quickly yanked the in-ear monitors out, answering it.

"Hey, give me a sec, I'm still coming off-stage and I can't hear."

She quickly made her way down the hallway and slammed the door on her dressing room, locking it to give her some privacy.

"Okay, sorry, everybody was trying to stop me, and I flew right past them." She breathed heavily as she collapsed in the chair.

"I figured, but I wanted to be sure and get you before you got somewhere you might not have cell service. To be perfectly honest with you, I couldn't wait any longer to hear your voice." His voice was rough as he told her the last part.

"I've missed you too."

"Thank you for the earrings." She could hear the smile in his voice.

"Thank you for the PMS kit," she laughed.

They were quiet for a minute and then she forged

ahead. "I'm sorry that ended up the way it did. I know the two of us are going to have to learn how to be married, and I know we're going to have some growing pains. I know we're going to argue, but I don't want to ever go days without talking to you again."

"Me neither. I'm sorry as hell about that," he told her. "I had to cool off and get some perspective."

"I'm not saying that just about you, Garrett. I'm sorry about me too. I could have easily picked up the phone and called you too. I just wasn't sure if you wanted to hear from me."

"Always," he answered quickly. "I always want to fucking hear from you."

"Are you sure? You did hang up on me," she teased.

"Not one of my finer moments, but I guarantee, if you had called me right back, I would have answered."

"I was a little too raw for that," she admitted. It was easier to admit things when he couldn't see her face. Then he couldn't see the shame burning on it. They had to get better at dealing with arguments. Hanging up on each other would never be the answer.

"I was too, but I hate being angry with you."

She smiled, debating on whether she should tell him this part or not. "Shell said that we fight just to make up."

He laughed loudly over the line. "Shell might be damn right," he agreed. "The only problem is we never seem to be in the same place to make up."

"Such is our life," she sighed. "But not for too much longer." A plan was already being formed in her mind, and she wondered if she was going to be able to pull it off or not. Another one of her five days off was coming at the end of the next week. She wondered if she could surprise her husband with the help of Jared. It would be worth it.

"Four more weeks," he answered for her. "I have a countdown on my phone. It tells me every morning when I wake up."

"That's right, it'll be over before we know it," she whispered.

"Hannah," Shell yelled from outside the door. "We gotta go in fifteen."

"Alright, I'll be ready."

"I heard her," Garrett said before she could tell him that she had to go.

"I'll talk to you soon, and hopefully I'll sleep better tonight since I know we're okay."

"Yeah," he agreed. "I've slept for shit the past couple of days too. I kept wondering if you were going to send me divorce papers, and I got a little worried when those earrings were delivered."

That hit her like a shot to the chest. "No way, Garrett. I don't believe in marriage being easy, which means divorce is the absolute last option in my mind. I'm not giving up on us over a stupid fight."

"Good, because I don't know what I would do without you, and that's not me blowing smoke up your ass, babe. You've quickly become the most important person in my life, and if I lost you, I might as well just give it up, because I wouldn't make it."

"You don't have to worry about that, I promise. We were being dumb. We'll try not to do that from now on."

"Love you," he told her. "I know you gotta go. Know that I think about you all the time."

"Same here." She smiled, even though she knew he couldn't see her. "Love you."

As soon as she hung up and walked out of the room, she was already talking to Shell and making plans for her upcoming day off.

"Are you sure everything is ready?" Hannah asked Shell for what seemed like the hundredth time.

"Yes, Hannah, fuck."

"Was that necessary?"

"Yes, you're driving me up a damn wall. Jared is going to get Garrett on that plane without ruining the surprise, I promise you."

This was the first time she'd ever planned a true surprise trip, and she was understandably nervous. "Sorry I'm annoying."

"It's okay, I get that you're nervous, but you've gotta trust us. We promised to help you and it's going to work out."

Hannah nodded, taking a deep breath. They were exactly five hours from Huntington Beach on this stop of the tour. By plane, it was much less, and she wanted to see her husband in a bad way. Day off number three of the tour was tomorrow. The plan she had come up with would begin in a few hours, so long as Jared lived up to his part of the deal. "I have to go on," Hannah trailed off.

"I know, go rock this concert, and then Hannah-and-Garrett getaway day is in effect. I'll have everything ready for you, I promise."

There wasn't much that Hannah didn't trust Shell with, so she knew without a doubt that Shell would come through for her, it wasn't a question of that. She just hoped what had gone on a few weeks ago would not discourage Garrett from doing what she wanted him to. It would ruin the whole plan.

"Are you sure we should go to this bar?" Garrett asked Jared. "Last time I went to a bar, all hell broke loose."

"This is a fucking hotel bar, we should be fine."

"I hate that we're here on business and we're this close to Hannah," Garrett grumbled. It wasn't unusual for the record company to send them to help with negotiations for acts that they wanted to sign, but Garrett was pissed that they were this close and he wouldn't be able to see his wife.

"Did you tell her?" Jared asked as he ordered a Coke.

Garrett ordered a beer and a shot of whiskey. "Yeah, and she was as sad as me. I hate hearing that tone in her voice, man. It sucks."

"I bet. You're doing better with it than you were though. I have to give that to you. You aren't a mean-ass fuck anymore," Jared joked.

"I can't change it. I might as well make the best of it, because it's not going to be any better if I keep pushing. It's only going to succeed in pissing us both off and maybe pushing her away. That's not what I want. I want a successful marriage. I have to learn how to pick my battles."

"Damn," Jared laughed. "Look at you being all mature and shit."

"I still like to drink." He threw the shot back, grinning.

The two of them sat there for a little while, talking about everything and nothing at the same time. Jared's phone buzzed, and he glanced down at it. "Shit, I gotta go take this. It's Shell."

It was loud in the bar, so Garrett didn't think anything of him holding up a finger and walking out, the phone held tightly to his ear.

"Do you want another shot?" the bartender asked, seeing the empty shot glass.

"Sure," Garrett figured he might as well have a good time since they had been forced to come on this excursion.

"Do you want to start a tab?"

Garrett felt a hand on his thigh, immediately tensing. "You can put it on mine, and when you bring him one, can you bring me one too?"

He glanced over to the side, and a slow smile spread across his face. His wife took a seat next to him, setting her own glass on the bar next to his. "You heard the lady," Garrett told the bartender.

Hannah still wore her stage makeup, and her hair had been redone. She pushed it back behind her ear. "You come here often? I don't think I've ever seen you before."

He couldn't help the thrill that shot through him, knowing that she was here and it looked like he was going to get to spend time with her. "I'm here on business," he explained. "How about you?"

Her brown eyes scanned the room before she slipped

the hand on his thigh up higher, lighting cupping him through his jeans. "Pleasure." She smiled, running her tongue over her bottom lip. "Lots and lots of pleasure."

The bartender came back, placing their shots in front of them. "Should we toast to your pleasure?" he asked, squirming in his seat.

She leaned so close that her lips touch his ear. "I think we should toast to ours."

"Where is my wife and what have you done with her?" he groaned as she squeezed the hand that cupped him. He fought not to close his eyes against the pleasure, he didn't want everyone in the place to know what was going on beneath the cover of the bar top, and he was almost positive that anyone who could see his face would know.

"Your wife?" she questioned, a saucy smile on her face. She leaned back towards him. "I was thinking I could be a groupie again."

That was it, all it took for him to stop thinking clearly. "Throw the shot back with me, and then we are getting out of here," he told her through clenched teeth.

The look in his eyes was all she needed to know, it was what she had longed to see for weeks. She needed this closeness to him, to physically feel that he was there with her. She literally could not wait. Picking up the shot glass, she saluted him, and then poured it down her throat, relishing the burn, knowing that it would help her loosen up. It would help her be the woman she wanted to be with him. To be perfectly honest, she still wasn't comfortable in that role, but she was learning, and that's all that mattered.

He did the same to her, slamming the glass down on

the lacquered surface of the bar, and then fished out his wallet, throwing some money there. They couldn't even pretend anymore that they were going to need a tab. Like always, their chemistry was combustible, and he knew he had to get her away from watchful eyes. He had to have her. Garrett got up from the barstool and held his hand out to her. "Please tell me you have a room."

She held up the card in her hand. "I do."

Without another word, he dragged her out of the bar and towards the bank of elevators. He didn't touch her as they waited, and it drove her insane, but as soon as the doors opened and he pushed her inside, the no-touching rule was no longer in effect.

Chapter Nineteen

Garrett waited until the elevator doors closed, making sure that no one got on with them, before he turned on Hannah.

Hannah saw the look in his eyes and immediately started walking backwards. When her back hit the coolness of the paneling of the elevator, she knew she was in trouble. "We shouldn't do this," she whispered.

"Do what?" he asked, the hungry look absorbing every part of her body.

"This. In public."

"Do you see anyone else around?" he asked as he advanced on her. He felt like a hunter stalking his prey. In a few strides, he was close enough so that his body almost touched hers, but not quite. One hand slapped against the paneling next to her head, the other hung loosely at his side. "Am I making you nervous?" He heard her sharp intake of breath.

"No," Hannah answered as she nodded her head yes. She had no choice but to widen her stance as he got himself all up in her business.

"I think I am, but I think you like it." He leaned in,

whispering in her ear.

He was precisely right, but she wasn't ever sure that she would be able to voice those feelings out loud. It would always be a struggle. She grasped his waist as his lips brushed against the side of her neck. How long was this elevator ride?

"Should we find out?"

She wanted to ask him "find out what?" Her mind was going every which way, and she couldn't concentrate on what they were talking about. The only thing Hannah knew was that she wanted him to take care of the ache that raged inside of her. She wanted that closeness with him and the relief and comfort that only he could give her. Her question was answered when his other hand came around the front of her skirt, pushing it up so that he could get to her.

"What will I find here?" he whispered in her ear, his teeth pulling on the lobe of her ear.

It was hard to stay standing when her knees were weak and all she wanted to do was lie down on this floor and have him go at her. It was in bad taste, she knew, but she would do almost anything he asked her to do without a second thought. She trusted him that much. "Excitement," she breathed, biting her bottom lip to keep it from trembling.

Pulling aside the fabric that kept them apart, he groaned loudly. "Feels like much more than excitement to me." He moved his head so that their lips could meet, but before he could do the things he wanted to, the elevator dinged. "Is this our floor?"

Hannah blinked hard, yanking the skirt down so that she was covered, and pushed her hair back from her face. "Umm," she looked at the card in her hand and then the digital display that showed the floor number. "Yes, this is it, we're at the end of the hall," she told him.

"Lead the way, babe."

She had come back to herself some before she stepped out of the elevator and onto the carpeted floor of the hotel hallway. She glanced behind her as they exited the elevator; she still wore the heels that she'd worn on stage. As she walked down the hallway, she couldn't help but add an extra sway to her hips.

"Killin' me," Garrett told her as he walked behind her.

She chanced another glance back at him and saw that he had slowed, truly admiring what he saw in front of him. It was moments like this that made her so thankful. She knew that she would never have to worry or wonder if this man wanted her. Every time he looked at her, she could tell. It was there in his eyes, in the set of his lips, in the look of adoration on his face. She was truly blessed with the best husband ever, and she was almost positive that Shell was right. They fought just to make up. Making her way to the room she'd rented for this night and the next day, she swiped the card in front of it, breathing a sigh of relief when it flashed green at her. Within seconds, Garrett was behind her, pushing her inside.

"Fucking never thought we'd get here." He slammed the door behind them.

No mention was even made of the f-word as he picked her up against him, wrapping her legs around his waist.

"Wait, I didn't get a chance to take a shower after the

show, I had to come straight here. That's why I'm painted up like a two-dollar hooker," she grinned.

He threw his head back, laughing at her choice of words. "I never took you for a two-dollar hooker, babe. Maybe a ten-dollar one, but never a two-dollar." He winked. He still held her against him and took stock of where he was.

"The bedroom is in there, the bathroom should be over there." She pointed to a closed door on the left.

With long strides, he walked them over that way and burst through the closed door.

"You can put me down," she laughed.

"No, I can't. I don't wanna let you go," he told her as he let go with one hand, searching for the light switch. When he found it, he flipped it on, taking in the shower that stared back at them. It was glass and there was a bench seat. "Fuck yeah," he breathed.

He reached in and turned the water on and then set his glasses down on the counter.

"Aren't we going to get undressed?" she asked when he opened the door.

"We can do that just as easily in here." He carried her into the shower and finally set her down.

"These are really expensive shoes, Garrett," she breathed out as he pushed her back against the tile wall, his body enveloping hers.

"I'll buy you more, just like I'll buy you another shirt and skirt," he told her.

She didn't have to ask what he meant when his hands went to her shirt and ripped it down the middle, same with her skirt. She stood there in front of him, the water from the shower running down her body, her clothes hanging in pieces beside her.

"I wish you could see how you look right now." He ran a finger from her bottom lip down her chest; he hooked it into the cup of her bra, pulling it down. His eyes flashed to hers before they went back down to the skin he had exposed.

Hannah pressed her hands against the hard tile, afraid to touch him. If she touched him, she knew she would make a fool of herself and swoon at his feet. She couldn't let him know that he had that much power yet. Swallowing hard, her eyes followed the path of his finger as it circled the hard tip of her breast. She watched as he lowered himself in a standing push up to grasp the piece of flesh between his lips, using his teeth to toy with her. "Garrett," she ground out, she was sliding, falling against the slickness of the shower.

"Nope, you stay upright," he told her, taking one hand off the tile and securing it to her hip. "I'll help you, baby, if you can't do it yourself."

She circled her arms around his neck, leaning her head back against the cool tile. Her body was on fire and she wanted him to put out the flames, that's all she wanted him to do. She didn't want him to toy with her anymore. Hannah closed her eyes against the sensations that were coursing through her. "I can't take it." Her breathing was shallow.

"You have to, I'm not done with you yet," he told her, insinuating himself between her thighs.

"No, I can't." She pressed herself tightly against his body. When he didn't pay attention to what she was saying, she unhooked one hand from around his neck and trailed it down her body. This was the first time she had ever been this bold with him, but they were married—she could be as bold as she wanted to. That's what he kept preaching to her, that there was no reason that either one of them should be embarrassed about anything they wanted to do with the other person. Using her hand, she pushed the cotton of her underwear aside and used the tips of her fingers to give her the relief that he wasn't.

"Hannah, that's gonna make me lose it," he warned her through gritted teeth, leaning his head against the tile. Even in the heels, he still towered over her.

"Good," she moaned against his neck. The way they stood put her at the perfect height and she took advantage of it. She used her teeth and mouth to put what she hoped were visible marks there. After the pictures with the other woman, she wanted everyone to know that he was hers.

He reached down, wrenching his belt lose at the buckle and pushing all his clothing down. Garrett grabbed her around the waist and lifted her so that her legs went around him, her ankles crossing and the heels of her shoes digging into his bare skin. "You keep that hand right there." He pushed against her, groaning when he felt the smooth skin of her palm stroke him while she stroked herself. He leaned forward, devouring her mouth with his, wanting her to know exactly how much he had been missing her, missing this, and how connected he felt to her when they showed their physical love to one another.

"God, Garrett." She gripped his hair with her other hand, ripping his lips from hers so that she could take a breath.

"I know." He withdrew and pushed back in, setting a punishing rhythm for the two of them. It had never been like this for him with any other woman he'd ever had, and he'd had a lot. There was no reason to lie, but there was something about the woman in his arms, and it wasn't just the fact that she wore his ring, it was something physical that drew her to him. It made him want to be with her all the time, made him want to bring her pleasure before himself. It made him want to be the giving sort of man that he always imagined a husband would be. "You feel so good," he praised her. "Hot and warm against me." His lips met her chin, tilting it up so that he could feast on her neck.

The way he spoke lulled her into a dream world where all that mattered was the feel of him entering and exiting her body and the feel of her own hand on her core. Hannah couldn't even hear the shower anymore, could barely feel the beating down of the water on them. At some point the other cup of her bra had come loose. That was her undoing, the feel of her sensitive flesh rubbing against his.

Garrett crushed her against him, a sound she had never heard ripping from somewhere deep inside him. His hips flexed against hers until it started to hurt and she had to move her legs.

"I can't feel my thighs anymore," she told him, breathing deeply, trying to get her panting under control.

"Sorry, shit, sorry," he told her, carefully unwrapping her legs, holding her up as she stood on the wet surface.

"Can you take the heels off?" she asked, pushing her hair back from her face, running a hand up her neck, surprised at how responsive her skin still was.

He leaned down, taking the heels off and placing them on the bench before having a seat himself. His heart was beating out of his chest. "I think you gave me a goddamn heart attack," he grinned over at her.

"Me?" she laughed. "That was all you, buddy."

Reaching over, he grabbed her around the waist and pulled her to him, sitting her on his lap. "I love the hell out of you, don't forget that."

"I know." She pushed his wet hair out of his eyes. It was getting much longer than normal. "I love you too."

Chapter Twenty

"What are we going to do today?" Hannah asked Garrett as they sat at the table in their hotel room, enjoying their breakfast.

"We really need to do something besides spend the whole day here, in bed."

"Yes, we do. Although I'm not sure what this place has to offer us."

"Me neither," Garrett sighed, pulling his phone over to him. He fiddled around for a few minutes. "Not a damn thing. This is the most boring town on the planet."

"We could hang here, I do have some things I need to do," she told him. "But we can't spend all day in bed." She smiled.

He smiled a slow smile back at her. "Are you sure?"

"Very. We get used to that and then what are we going to do for the next few weeks?"

She had a point, he had to give her that. "I have some writing for the next session we have to get done. How about I call Jared and see what he and Shell are up to."

"Sounds good," she nodded. "I've got a few things I

can write on too. Even if we're only in the same hotel room, I'm fine with that. I just want to be around you until I have to leave."

"Me too." He leaned over and kissed her softly on the lips.

She finished eating her breakfast and then went to the bathroom to freshen up. Lying on the bench were her beloved high heels. After she brushed her teeth and put her hair up in a ponytail, making sure that everything Garrett had done to her the night before was completely covered, she walked out, shoes in hand. "I think you owe me a new outfit."

He wore a shit-eating grin as he made his way over to where she stood. "Seems like you're right. Do I get to pick out the outfit, or do you?"

"Don't really care about the outfit, babe," she teased him, calling him what he normally called her. "I do care about the shoes, they better well be the same exact ones. I'm giving you these for reference. You don't want to see my southern crazy come out if they aren't the same."

He watched her, his eyes narrowed. "Are you trying to tell me they've been discontinued and I'm gonna have to give my left nut to get a pair of them?"

"You are so crude sometimes. No they aren't discontinued, but they are very expensive. They were my treat to myself when my first song went number one. I didn't have the money to buy these, but I bought them anyway. They cost me a month's rent, if that tells you anything."

"I happen to think that the time we had together was worth it. I don't know about you..." he trailed off.

"Oh, I never said it wasn't worth it. My favorite thing in the world is when you lose control and you take me any way you want to. I love that." She ran her hand down his arm, clasping their fingers together. "But I loved these shoes too. They've seen me through some very hard times."

"I can show you some very hard times," he mumbled, just loud enough for her to hear.

"I'm serious, Garrett."

"Oh, I am too, like a week ago." He laughed when she slapped him in the chest. He captured her hand and brought it to his lips.

"Stop trying to be sweet after being crude." She wrinkled her nose.

"You know you love it."

She opened her mouth to answer him but was interrupted by a knock on the door. Walking over, she opened it, seeing Jared and Shell on the other side. "Hi." She waved at them.

Shell thrust a frappe at her, a smile on her face. "Figured you might need this today."

"I love you," Hannah laughed, closing her eyes and taking a drink from the cold beverage.

"I have to admit I had ulterior motives."

Hannah took a good look at her friend, and noticed that she wasn't as happy as she should have been after spending the night with her boyfriend.

"Don't be a Debbie Downer," Garrett yelled from where he sat at the table.

"What's going on?" Hannah asked, her stomach clenching for some reason. It was too much that they be happy for longer than a few hours. That was the way this tour was going.

"Have you been on your phone or anything today?"

Garrett groaned from where he sat. "Not something else. For fucking real, can't we all just be happy for one day?"

"I honestly wouldn't say anything about this, but I know it's going to upset and piss her off in a very big way."

Hannah closed her eyes. "Can you tell me? Maybe it will be better coming from you."

Jared reached over, putting his hand on Shell's shoulder for support while she searched to find the words. "The record company put out an alternate version of your new song. It's a duet with Bryson Grant." Silence greeted her announcement and that made Shell nervous. "Please say something."

"What is there to say? How did they do this? Why did they do this? I didn't even record with him." Hannah was beginning to panic, they could all see it in her face, could tell it in the way her breath was coming quickly, in short pants.

Garrett got up from where he sat. "Babe, calm down. Come on, let's sit down."

"Why aren't you upset about this?" Her eyes cut to Garrett. "I wanted you on this song." Tears pooled and her face broke.

"Shit." Garrett pulled her into his arms. "It's okay, I'm not mad," he told her, enveloping her in his arms.

"I am," she sobbed. "How dare they do this to me? I was very clear in what I would and would not do about this song. How could they do this? I wrote this song for you, that's why I was so upset. How could he do this to me? I thought he was my friend."

"Han, they probably did to him what they did to

you." Shell had a seat next to her friend and put her hand on Hannah's arm. "I'm willing to bet he recorded his own version, you recorded yours, and they put them together. Don't be so quick to throw Bryson under the bus."

Angry didn't even begin to cover how upset she was at this news. Glancing around the room, she saw what she had to work with and knew what she had to. "You know what? I'll record my own version and upload it online then." She sniffed, shrugging as if it wasn't a big deal.

"What do you mean?" Shell asked, not understanding.

"I have the person here that I wanted to sing the song with, we have a guitar player, and you would make a phenomenal camera woman. Why can't I do what I wanted to do in the first place?"

They all looked at one another, realizing that Hannah was right. They had everything they needed to make a video to upload to YouTube or wherever else they wanted to upload it to.

"Alright." Garrett shrugged. "Let me learn the words. Jared, you got your guitar?"

"Don't go anywhere without it. Let me go back to our room and get it."

"You don't know the words yet?" Hannah glared over at her husband. She'd sent him the song a few weeks ago.

Garrett's face blushed a deep red. "I've been busy."

"Hmmm." She shot him another look.

"Do not judge me." He pointed a finger at her. "I love your stuff, but I have been very busy."

She finally let the smile break over her face, wiping the tears away. "You're cute when you're trying to get in my good graces."

"Woman, I just got there, I don't need to go back to the dog house." He got up. "I'm gonna go with Jared. If he's got another guitar, I might be able to play with him."

Hannah glanced over at Shell; she was already setting up her computer, pulling up the video editors she had on there. "Do you think this is a good idea?"

Shell looked up and shrugged. "You have to stand up for yourself, no matter what that means, no matter how. If you keep letting them walk all over you, then they will. I have to admit that I think this is a super low blow. You were very adamant in the fact that you absolutely did not want to do this with Bryson, and they went behind your back anyway. As bad as it sounds, they deserve whatever they get."

"You think I'll get in trouble?"

"I think you're a songwriter who should be able to perform her song in any way she sees fit. If that's in a hotel room with her husband and a guitarist, then you should be allowed to do that," Shell sighed. "They're used to jerking you around because they can. If you do this, then they know they can't anymore, and you've taken a huge step in your desire to be free of all the chains. I'm proud of you for this."

"Thank you." Hannah reached over, hugging her friend.

"Now do I think we'll both get a stern talking to? Yes, so we might as well go ahead and be prepared for it."

The guys came back then, both carrying guitars. Hannah busied herself with getting the original lyrics and sheet music out of her bag, setting it down in front of them. She had never been a part of the actual music process and was excited to see Jared look at the music and begin to play it. Garrett took a little while longer to catch up on it.

"You got it," Jared told him as Garrett struggled with a chord progression. "Put your middle finger here." He indicated by moving his own fingers. "It'll make it easier on you to switch."

Garrett did what Jared told him and they continue to play. The first couple of times it was sloppy, and Garrett had more than a few mistakes. He glanced up at Hannah, his face red with embarrassment. "It takes me a few times, usually." He gave her lopsided grin.

"You're still better than me, I can't even play chord progressions," she told him. "The question is can you play and sing at the same time."

Jared laughed from where he sat. "She called you on that one. *Can* you sing and play at the same time?"

"Yes, fucker." He threw one of the papers at Jared.

"Shell, you should sing some harmony for us," Hannah told her.

"Wait a second." Jared glanced over at her, surprise on his face. "She can sing?"

"Not well," Shell laughed. "But I can harmonize. I do it with her all the time. I'm on most of the singles. I tend not to ask for a lot of publicity for it because I'm not great at it."

"She's a very good harmonizer, but she's very shy about it," Hannah was saying. "That's why I'm trying to get her to do it."

"If it'll get you to shut up, then I'll gladly do it."

"Great!" Hannah beamed.

The group of them got ready, situated themselves, and then Shell hit record. It took them a few takes—Garrett messed up the chords once, Hannah messed up the lyrics twice, trying to keep from laughing, and then Shell erased what they had considered their best performance. Finally, they got it all together, and by the end of the song, Hannah had tears in her eyes. There was something that she loved about singing with Garrett, and when he looked at her like she was the only person in the world, it solidified that she was exactly where she needed to be.

"Let's get this uploaded," Shell clapped. "I can't wait to see how many views it has by the end of the night. I can almost guarantee it will out-view Bryson's version."

"I hate to do that to him, but sometimes I gotta do what I gotta do." Hannah folded her arms over her chest.

"He'll get it. Hell, I think everybody will get it once they see this. If you could see it from my point of view." Shell shook her head. "It's beautiful."

Hannah couldn't wait, and she was excited to see what the fans would think of it. As far as the record company went, she could care less; they hadn't cared about her wishes. It was time for her to do what she wanted to and what she knew would be best for her family. Screw anyone who stood in her way.

Chapter Twenty-One

"Well, it took seven days, but I finally got my nasty gram," Hannah told Shell as the two of them sat on the tour bus making their way back towards the Midwest.

"About uploading that video?"

"Yeah, I was waiting on it." She shifted in her seat and pulled the laptop closer to her. "Figured it would have been before now."

Shell stood up and came to stand behind her, reading over her shoulder. "They are so damn condescending," Shell laughed.

"I know, but I checked with legal, there's nothing they can do to me. I own the song, I wrote it, and it's published under my company. They can only express their displeasure." She clapped her hands. "This not-doing-what-I'm-supposed-to thing is getting to be fun."

"Wonder what took them so long?"

"I guarantee you they were looking for a way to screw me over. I'm not letting them do it again. The holidays are coming up; I want to spend time with my husband and my family. I'm not letting them put a damper on it. We end this tour the week before Thanksgiving. I am going to spend my first married Thanksgiving with my husband, and then hopefully I'll spend Christmas in my brand new house." She ran her hand through her hair.

"How's that going by the way?"

"We close next week. I'm faxing the paperwork in because I can't be there and neither can Garrett. It's kind of sad. Dad's going to go over and make sure everything's okay and oversee the changing of the locks and stuff. Then we'll transfer my house into your name." She grinned.

Things were moving ahead on all fronts, and for that she was excited. She couldn't handle anything else going wrong.

"You still holding up okay? Physically and mentally?" Shell asked. She tried to make it a point to ask now, just because of what their friendship had gone through over the years. If Hannah got overwhelmed, it wasn't good for either of them.

"I am. I weigh in with Garrett tonight, actually." She checked the calendar. "I think I might be running on the skinny side, but it's not from lack of effort, we're just freakin' busy."

"Don't I know that. If he gives you shit, tell him to call me. I got your back on this one."

Hannah giggled, and then settled deeper into the seat. November was coming in cold in the Midwest, and she could see frost on the window. She hugged the hoodie that she wore closer to her body; they still had a few hours before they would reach their destination for the night. "I haven't asked in a long time, because I don't want to make you feel like you have to talk to me about it. I have to admit though, I'm curious. How are things going with Jared?"

"It's much different than your relationship with Garrett." Shell played with a string on the PJ pants she wore. "Sometimes I don't necessarily know where I stand with him, other times I think he loves me."

"Has he told you that yet?" With anyone else, Hannah wouldn't have asked, but this was her best friend. They shared everything that they could.

Shell shook her head, biting her bottom lip. "No."

"Aww, honey, I'm sorry."

"I've told him." Shell shrugged. "But he's never said it back. It sucks putting yourself out there like that and your feelings not being returned."

"How do you know they aren't returned? Maybe Jared has a hard time expressing them. Not every guy is like Garrett. I lucked out in a big way. I'm very lucky." As she said the words, she realized how true they were.

"You deserve it."

Hannah shook her head. "Not any more than you do. You deserve it too."

"It's not that he's mean to me or that I doubt his feelings, not really. I know I mean a lot to him. He calls me every day, no matter if he's having a good day or a bad day. He still has bad days, although they are few and farther between now. That means everything to me, that I'm the person who he wants to talk to, to bring him back from that ledge. I don't get the feeling that he's had much love in his life from anyone besides Garrett, the guys, and Garrett's family." Shell worried that she was overstepping her boundaries, but she had to talk to someone about this, and Hannah was her best friend in the whole world.

"Why do you think that?" Hearing what her friend said made Hannah's heart hurt. No matter where she was in the world—in her addiction, in her attitude—she always knew she was loved. Her parents had made sure of that. To know that there was someone she was close to who didn't have that hurt.

"Some of the things he's said. He doesn't come right out and say his parents were assholes to him, but there have been little hints here and there. I've also heard a few things that Garrett's parents have said when they think no one is listening. I get the feeling that Jared was a hard child for his parents to love." She was delicate in how she worded it.

"That's BS we both know it." Hannah thumped her finger on the table. "Children are not hard to love."

"For us, no, but we don't know the circumstances. I'm trying so hard to not be judgy."

"Have you met them yet?" Hannah tried to rack her brain. Come to think of it, no one had ever mentioned Jared's parents other than in passing.

"When would I meet them?"

"You think they would care since their son cares."

Shell sighed. "That's the root of it—I wonder if he does."

"I thought you said that he does, he just hasn't expressed it."

"I don't know what I mean!" Shell ran her hand through her hair. This obviously bothered her a lot more than she let on.

"Why don't you cut the crap and tell me what's really

going on here?" Hannah raised her eyebrows at her friend, sick of talking in circles. "We both know if you didn't want to talk about it, you would have told me to mind my own."

"Fine. Why do you have to be so fucking observant?"

"I know you and I love you. You listen to me gripe and complain about everything all the time. It's only fair that I listen to you. I'm here for you just like you're here for me. Tell me what's going on."

Tears came to Shell's eyes, and it was as uncharacteristic for Shell as cursing was for Hannah. It scared Hannah; obviously her friend had been going through some things and kept them quiet.

"I don't know how much longer I can do this," she whispered.

Do what? As far as Hannah knew things were going great with the other couple. There never seemed to be any tension when they all hung out as a group. "What are you doing?"

"Coming second to what he really wants. Every day is a serious struggle for him, and I don't know that I'm enough to keep him from wanting to go back to the drugs. I don't know that I'm strong enough to handle it, and I don't know if I'm strong enough to pull him back." She breathed a sigh of relief, almost like that had been weighing her down for a long time.

"That's not your job, Shell. You've gotta get it through your head that you aren't his reason for not using; you are his reason for living his life. He's got to want to not use, and that's no reflection on you. That's all on him. Has he blamed this on you?" she asked, her temper flaring.

"No, but I see him struggle and I blame it on myself. What if I was around more? What if I was able to answer the phone every time he called? What if I was available at all hours of the day? Would I be able to stop it?"

"Listen to me," Hannah's voice was sharp and clear, probably clearer than she'd ever heard it before. "You can't take his struggle on. You won't do him any good if you do. If you are available all the time and at his beck and call, guess what? He's going to become addicted to you. He's an addict, Shell. That's what he does. Don't become another addiction. You're his salvation by showing him that there is something else out there, that if he works hard enough at it, he can have a normal life. He needs that; he needs to know what normal is."

"I feel like I'm a stepping stone to something better. That once he feels like he's clean enough, he's going to move on."

Hannah had never known Shell to suffer from low self-esteem in her life; this was all new to her. "Stop that nonsense right now. Jared loves you. He might not be able to put those feelings into words, but I see the way he looks at you, and he loves you. Give him time."

"How much fucking time does he need?"

Hannah winced. "Have you talked to him about this?"

"No, hell no. That's awesome, tell your boyfriend, 'I'm not sure whether you love me or not, because I've said it and you haven't.' How well is that going to go over?"

"It's life. We ask questions because we want to know answers," Hannah laughed.

"I'm not there yet. Maybe with a few beers in me over the holidays, I'll do it," she sighed. "Thanks for listening. I miss our gab sessions."

"I do too. We'll have to make it point to have a few more of them."

Shell opened her mouth but was cut off by the ringing of Hannah's phone. "That's Garrett, go have fun talking to your hubby."

"I can tell him I'll call him back later. You were here before Garrett."

"Take the call, I'll be good. It helped that you listened."

Hannah answered, asking Garrett to hang on. She got up, hugging her friend. "No matter what, *I* love you." She didn't wait for Shell to answer, but instead made her way back to her bedroom.

Shell sat there, battling tears and the feeling that arose whenever she allowed herself to think about how far they had come and how far they had to go. She wouldn't give up on Jared, but she also hoped she wouldn't give up on herself.

Chapter Twenty-Two

Hannah had a seat on her bed, holding the phone in front of her.

"You ready to weigh-in, babe?" Garrett asked her.

She tilted her head and smiled. His hair was getting even longer than when she'd seen him a week ago. It was obvious he hadn't shaved in a few days, and he wore a tank top over his body. She could see that he was sweating and red; he'd probably just got done working out. Good grief, she missed him in a bad way.

"I guess so, but I'm warning you now, the pace we're keeping is exhausting. Shell told me that if I'd lost and you give me crap, to let her know, she can vouch for me."

Garrett glanced at her. "I can tell you're tired. I'm sorry, babe, so damn sorry that you're wearing yourself out like this. I wish there was some way I could change it or make it better."

"I have a couple more weeks. When I see you after performing that last show, I want to sleep for two days straight. Do not bother me."

He was amused at the way she said it. "I can't help

but bother you a little. I have to show my love some-how."

"You know what I mean, Garrett," she sighed.

"You're done, aren't you?"

She nodded. "I am, and I hate to say that because I have never wanted to be off a tour this much in my life. I feel like I'm not giving my all to these fans that have come out and seen me."

"No, babe, I've read the reviews. They are killer. You're giving it everything you've got, and I think that's why you're so tired. You're overcompensating."

Was he right? Was she purposely tiring herself out so that no one could say that she wasn't giving it her all? The thought held weight, but honestly she was too tired to even think about it at this point. The only thing she could be focused on was the fact that she had a few more weeks to go. Wanting to take her mind off of it, she forged ahead. "Did you get the info from the real estate attorney about our closing next week?"

"Yes, and I am very excited. I really appreciate your dad going over and taking care of all the stuff we can't. I sent him a message."

"You sent my dad a message?" The surprise was evident in her voice.

"What? You act like we don't talk. He and I text regularly. We're not up each other's asses like you are with my mom," he fired back. "Telling secrets on me and finding out about all the shit I did when I was younger."

She laughed. "Stop being bitter."

"God, I miss you," he sighed.

She smiled softly at the face across the screen from

her. "I miss you too, but we can't let this get us down. Before I weigh, I wanna talk to you about something, though."

He tilted his head to the side. "Is this gonna be a good conversation or a bad conversation? I can't tell by the way you presented it. I'm thinking it can be either-or."

"Stop. I don't set you up for bad ones, no matter what you think."

He chuckled and a smile spread across his face. "Alright, alright, what do we need to conversate about?"

"Jared and Shell."

"Oh, hell no." He held his hand up. "I am not talking to you about our best friends' relationship."

"Garrett, she's upset."

He sighed dramatically. He did not want to be a part of this. He had learned a long time ago not to get involved in his friend's romantic life, but unfortunately it looked like she hadn't. "Then they need to work that out together."

"Can you hear me out? Please? I have some questions that I need answered."

He squirmed. "I don't like this, Han."

"You don't have to like it; I'm the one doing the asking. You can throw me under the bus if you need to."

He hoped to God she remembered that she'd said that, because the one thing Jared hated was people gossiping about him—didn't matter if it was about his everyday life or his love life. He was one of the most private people that Garrett knew. "Okay, what is it?"

"How was his childhood? Shell said that she's thrown the L-word out and he's not responded, but she kind of got that his childhood wasn't the best."

He sighed. He didn't want to go into this with her, but he had already opened himself up to it. "His childhood wasn't the best. It's part of the reason why he's always struggled with the drugs."

"Can you elaborate on it? I'd like to know how to help her."

Garett had never had to tell his wife that something was none of her business, but he was tempted to tell her that now. At what point did he betray a best friend and keep a wife? He wasn't sure. "I don't know that I'm comfortable with this, Han."

"I don't want you to do something that you don't want to do, but she's hurting."

"He hurts every day," he fired back at her. "He had two pieces-of-shit for parents. They didn't give one damn about him and, luckily, mine did. That's all anyone needs to know. Nobody told him that they loved him until he came to stay with me. He has a very hard time expressing his feelings because he was never shown how to. I can tell you beyond a shadow of a doubt, though, that he cares a lot for her. More than he's ever cared for anyone else. I know that because he's been clean since they started dating. He's never been clean for anyone else. Not even for me. She has a huge impact on him, and if he's willing to give up snorting shit through his nose for her, then that's love."

"Okay, I just wanted to make sure he wasn't going to break her heart," Hannah hurried to cut him off.

"Just because he loves her doesn't mean he's not going to break her heart. I think we both know that." He hated all this feeling nonsense that wasn't about the two of them. It felt like he was going behind Jared's back. He didn't want Jared to feel the way he had when he found out that Stacey and Brad were dating. "That's all I'm saying about it. Seriously, I'm not gossiping about it anymore. Shell is a big girl, and she knows what she's gotten into with him, otherwise she wouldn't be where she is now."

"That's true, but sometimes you need to hear how the other person feels."

"Han." His voice was firm. "I said drop it. I can't make Jared be more open with his feelings any more than you can. We just have to hope that they can work through it. It's not about what's best for us; it's about what's best for them. If Shell can handle it, then she can. If she can't, then she can't."

"Alright," she sighed. "I want them to be as happy as we are."

"Not everybody can have that, babe," he laughed. "Now get your ass on the scale."

She was nervous about this, to be honest. She was eating, but she noticed that her clothes were getting looser. The pace they were keeping was tiring, and she knew that she was losing more weight than she was putting on. It wasn't an obsession, she knew that, but she hoped that he would too. Hannah got on, announcing her weight out loud.

"That's two pounds less than last week. You've gotta step up your caloric intake," he told her, his tone back to serious.

"I don't know what else to do." She sat down on the bed. "I've never kept up this kind of intense pace before. I'm going back for seconds at night, and I'm doing my best to even eat a real breakfast and not just a couple of pieces of toast like normal. I'm ordering omelets and bacon on the side."

Garrett ran a hand through his hair. "Have you thought about meal supplements? You wouldn't have to do them forever, but you could drink them in between. They would give you enough calories to put back on the seven total pounds you've lost."

"I wouldn't even know where to begin," she told him, frustration obvious in her voice.

"Let me take care of it."

She was good with that. Anything that she didn't have to worry with in this stage of the tour she was all for. For the next few weeks, she was solely focused on getting done and over with so that she could spend the holidays with her family.

"Okay, just send me a list, or whatever."

"Are you doing okay besides being tired as hell?" Garrett asked sincerely, wanting to make sure that she was okay mentally.

"Yeah," she breathed deeply. "I have two more days off, and I know that we try to see each other, but I'm thinking it might be best if I try to sleep on those days. I'm getting very tired, and I had a scratchy throat when I woke up this morning. That's the last thing I need, to be sick."

"What if I come to you?" He didn't relish going a few more weeks without seeing her.

"Well," she lay down, positioning herself on the bed, "if you come to me, then that's a whole other ballgame, but I can't be flying like I have been. I don't want to come off the tour and be sick for three weeks."

He didn't want that either. "When is your next day off?"

"Umm." She reached over and grabbed her calendar. "I have next Thursday and the following Monday off, then the tour ends that Thursday. I don't know why they did it that way, but who am I to ask?"

They were so close to be being done that Garrett could taste it. He couldn't wait. "How about I come see you next Thursday, and then I'll be there the following Thursday night—the last night of the tour?"

"That would be amazing because it would help me get the tour stuff done, and if I'm too tired, you can handle it." She gave him a bright smile.

"I don't know about all of that, but I'll do what I can to help."

They said their goodbyes and got off the phone. Hannah was feeling great about the next few weeks and beyond. She was feeling great until Shell walked in, a grim look on her face.

"Bryson made a statement."

The way Shell said it made Hannah's stomach drop. She wasn't sure what that statement was, she had no idea the words that had come out of his mouth, but she was more than positive that she wasn't going to like them.

Chapter Twenty-Three

Hannah had fumed all night after she read the statement that Bryson had given to the press.

"I'm really proud of the song that Hannah and I made. I'm upset that she went behind my back and recorded another version with another artist."

She had thought for hours about what she wanted to do, what she wanted to say. And even if she could only be honest to herself, it had really ticked her off that Bryson had said another artist. Garrett was her *husband*.

It wasn't until then that she'd logged onto YouTube and found that her and Garrett's version of the song had already been seen by over four million people. She glanced at the version with Bryson and saw that it hadn't even reached a million yet. After she'd looked at the views, she'd steeled herself and looked at the comments. It had been a very long time since she had made herself do that, and she'd almost backed out, but what she found amazed her. Almost every single comment on her and Garrett's version was supportive, while what was on her and Bryson's were not.

It seemed that a lot of people were just as ticked as

she had been that they'd released a love song with someone besides her husband. Those comments and the unsolicited support was what made her finally take a seat at the table on the tour bus. Her laptop sat in front of her, camera ready to go. She was going to make her own statement. At this point, she didn't care. Like she'd told Shell, it was becoming fun going against everything that everyone expected her to do and be. She checked her reflection in the camera and situated herself on the seat before pressing record.

"Hey, Harmony fans!" She waved, smiling brightly into the camera. "I wanted to take a minute to address the comments made by Bryson Grant." She took a few seconds, composing herself and trying to think up the best way she could say what she felt, but not being crass at the same time.

"He and I have been friends since we were in high school, so it surprised me to read what he said. While I know it could very easily have been taken out of context, I felt like I needed to respond. I wrote the song in question for my husband—it is one hundred percent about him and the love I feel for him. When the record company wanted me to do a duet, I said no to anyone but Reaper. I can't fake how I feel, even if it is just to sing. He's my husband and the love of my life. If I'm going to sing that kind of song, it's only ever going to be with him."

She stopped for a second, tilting her head to the side. "I know that a lot of you will understand that and realize that I'm taking my break in a couple weeks to spend time with him so that we can be normal for a while. Having said that, when the record company went behind *my* back and released a spliced-together version of the song, I was understandably upset. Since I *am* the owner of the song, I did it the way I wanted to. Reaper and I greatly appreciate the support and the views of the song on YouTube. Call and request it at your local radio stations, we'd love to see a grassroots campaign start." She winked, smiling wickedly.

"Thank you for the support, and I love you! I won't forget any of you on my break. Hopefully, you won't forget me." She waved at the camera before turning it off.

A slow clap could be heard behind her and she turned around, seeing Shell standing there. "That was a really great explanation of what's going on. You even kind of, but not really, threw the record company under the bus. You did it with a smile on your face. What have you done with my Hannah?"

Hannah giggled. "She got stronger."

"I'm proud of you." Shell hugged her close. "Want me to upload this for you?"

"Please, I'm still not a whiz at that, and I don't want to accidentally delete it before it gets out there. I don't know that I have the guts to make that statement again."

Shell smirked. "Out of curiosity, have you said anything to Bryson?"

"I am so flippin' angry with him," Hannah started, before gripping her water bottle so that it made a loud noise. "I mean, where does he get off?"

"You know it's probably what the record company told him to say."

"No, I know Bryson; I've known him a long time." She shook her head. "He's never been a puppet, and he never says anything that he doesn't mean. He said what he wanted to. I'm thinking that maybe the record company told him that I was good with us recording this song together and he got the wrong idea. How? I don't know, but weirder things have happened. I might text him, but I'm too ticked right now."

"Chances are he'll text you before you text him because the statement you just made was the best 'kiss my ass' I've heard in a long time."

The two women looked at each other and then broke out into giggles. Hannah laughed so hard she cried, feeling relief for the first time in weeks. The stress that weighed so heavily down on her broke a little, and it felt good. "I'm kind of excited that I did it," she admitted. "It felt good to tell people how I really feel, and I think it might actually be well received. You should see the comments in support of Garrett and me on our YouTube video. I'm surprised as all get-out."

"Why? People always root for love."

Hannah snorted. "Not always. You know that some fans have been wishy-washy about us being together. I think the record company just fixed it for us though. Now those fans will want to root for people who are sticking it to the man."

Shell laughed. "I can't believe you used the term 'the man'," she giggled. "I know I shouldn't be finding all this funny, but I love the woman you've become, lady. You make my job damn interesting."

"What can I say?" Hannah shrugged. "I'm not content with doing what I'm told anymore. I want my life to be my own."

"Did you happen to see that you're charting on a *country* chart?"

Garrett's eyebrow shot up at the words that came out of Jared's mouth. "No...what the fuck?"

"That video we made in a hotel room of you and Hannah singing that song is going viral. It's charting. Radio stations are ripping the vocals and playing it on the radio. Especially after the statement she released earlier today," Jared told him, clicking on Hannah's YouTube page.

"I saw earlier that she'd said something. I haven't watched it yet, though."

"Well you need to, 'cause your meager little wife stood up to everybody and grabbed them by the balls. I'm pretty proud of her." Jared clapped his best friend on the shoulder. "Mrs. Thompson has come a long way."

Garrett laughed. "Thanks, buddy, it's all my influence."

"Keep dreamin'." Jared smacked him in the stomach.

"Have you heard anything from our label?" Brad asked. Normally he didn't get involved in the married couple's business, but this could affect them as a band.

"I got a message from Rick earlier," Garrett answered. Rick was their touring manager, who had in the past few months become their official manager. "He said that at first the higher-ups weren't sure what to do with it because we didn't get permission, but that our backlist had started selling on iTunes and they were choosing to turn a blind eye to it as of now. Will they continue? I don't know, but I don't care either. She took a huge step in doing that, and there's no way that I can take that away from her, ya know?"

Brad nodded. "I'd have to agree with you there. She did take a huge step, and for someone like her, that unknown was a big one. I'm proud of her too."

"I hope everyone knows this doesn't mean we're doing a country album, though," Jared shivered. "No way in hell am I wearing a pair of tight jeans, cowboy hat, or cowboy boots. Fuck that."

"I think we all agree that there will be none of that in this band," Garrett laughed. "C'mon, let's get this song done. Two more and then we turn it in."

"You nervous?" Brad asked.

They had all decided to go with Hannah's suggestion that they make the record they want to and forget what the label wanted. None of them had talked about how they felt it would be perceived.

"A little," Jared admitted. "I mean, disappointing the label is still like disappointing family, but I think in the end they'll grow to like it. We believe in what we're doing. We have to stay strong and true to that."

Garrett nodded. "A-fucking-men. If we had been scared when we first started out, we wouldn't have gotten anywhere. We can't lose that. If we lose that, then we'll never do the things we want to again. As a group, we still have to have that little bit of fuck-you in us. We still have to have that little bit of not doing what we're supposed to."

"Then get your ass in the booth and give them the biggest fuck-you you got." Their engineer pointed at Garrett. "Let's get this shit done."

That night as she came off-stage, Shell handed Hannah her phone. The first thing she always did was look for a text from Garrett. When she saw that she had a new one, she was excited and unlocked it to see who it was from.

"Huh? Wonder what Bryson is texting me for?"

"Probably because of your statement." The *duh* was left out of Shell's words, but it was heard.

"I figured he would have said something by now. What took him so long?" She shrugged, opening up the message. As she read it, her face burned.

> *"How dare you put me in the position of making you more famous than you already are and using me to make other people accept your marriage to your husband? I thought we were friends, Hannah. That song was supposed to be ours, you promised."*

She had no idea who had promised, it definitely hadn't been her, and reiterated the fact that she thought someone at the record company had set the two of them up. "He's mad." She tilted the phone towards Shell and let her read it.

"He has no right to be that angry. If someone at the record company promised it, then he needs to take it up with them. That pisses me off," Shell mumbled, walking with Hannah down the hall.

"How do I even respond to this? I feel bad that he seems to have gotten the short end of the stick, but there's also a part of me that doesn't care."

"I wouldn't respond, I'd let it go."

That didn't feel good to Hannah. She and Bryson

had known each other for a long time. She tried to think of how she would feel if someone blew her off like that. "It doesn't feel good to do that."

"I'm being honest with you. He's pissed. He's going to piss you off, and then he's going to say something that he doesn't mean, and it's going to make you mad. Without meaning to, you'll get Garrett involved, and then it will be a knock-down, drag-out between everyone. I think it's best to let it go. If he says something else, then you can answer it."

Maybe Shell was right, maybe she did need to let it go. It wouldn't change anything about her life now or after the tour was over. As far as she was concerned, her eyes were on the prize, and that prize was the Thursday before Thanksgiving. That's when she would be done, and that's when she could truly start living her life.

Chapter Twenty-Four

"**Y**ou've got a delivery from California."

Those were beginning to be Hannah's favorite words in the world. That meant that Garrett had taken the time to send her something. Sometimes it was little, other times it was big, like flowers. Today, she wasn't exactly sure what it was.

Shell sat a box down in front of her and waited patiently for her to open it. Hannah's gifts had become something that they both looked forward too. They each tried to guess what it was before she officially ripped into it.

"I'm not sure about this one," Hannah told Shell, tilting her head from side to side. "All the other ones have been self-explanatory, this one is a box."

"I gotta admit, I'm stumped too. Usually there's a rhyme and reason for what he's sending and we can get a good clue from how it looks wrapped, but this..." Shell trailed off.

Shrugging, Hannah tore in, wondering just what in the world she would find there. She tried to think back to the conversations that she and Garrett had been having lately. "I have no idea either," she said as she opened the box, laughing when she saw what was in there.

"What the hell is that?"

Hannah took a minute to examine it and then threw her head back laughing. "It's different meal replacement drinks. He told me after I weighed in the other day that I needed to slow down the weight loss." She pulled out the first one and saw it had a note attached to it. "Oh my God," she giggled.

"Did he make personal notes for you?" Shell asked as she scoped the writing that was attached to each bottle.

Flipping the carton around in her hand, she saw that he had. "It looks like he taste-tested them for me," she laughed. "He's insane."

"About you, and it's super cute." To say that Shell was a little jealous was an understatement, but it would do her no good to talk about it.

"He'll be here the day after tomorrow and I'm excited."

Shell watched her friend. The excitement was noticeable in the way her eyes brightened, the smile on her face got bigger, and the tone of her skin. There was one thing that none of them had counted on with this marriage—how much it would help Hannah become the person they all knew had been inside her. It had helped her blossom, and Shell had never been happier. "I'm excited for you. I know these past few weeks haven't been easy."

"They haven't been easy on any of us. It's not only me, it's everybody. We've all worked our behinds off."

"That's true, but I think you've dealt with the brunt

of the stress. You're the one going out there killing it every night, when all you seriously want to do is be at home with your husband. I have to give it to you, I didn't know if you would be able to do these eight weeks, but you've been a trooper. I'm proud of you, Han."

She smiled. "Thanks, but I'm so ready to go home," she laughed. "But I'm going to suck it up, drink this meal replacement that says 'I rock' and hope for the best."

Truer words had never been spoken for all of them.

Shell loved mornings when she was the only one awake. The bus that she and Hannah occupied never had that many people in it, Hannah valued her privacy too much, but sometimes it was nice to be awake without Hannah. It was in those moments that she allowed herself to reflect on where she was in her life and do it alone. It was where she cried most of her tears and let her fears take hold. She never told those things or shared those feelings with anyone. It was her way of self-preservation.

This morning, she moved to the coffee maker and got her first cup before sitting down at the bar. In front of her on her laptop screen was the information that she needed to apply for the college program that she had been looking into. Scared didn't even begin to describe the way she was feeling. There had been points in her life where she hadn't been sure what she wanted to do, but this was a whole different ballgame. Hannah had told her what her own plans were, and for the first time, those didn't include Shell. It was time for her to realize and understand that maybe she would have to continue with something that didn't include the two of them. It had weighed heavily on her, after they had their talk, but Shell had made it a point not to dwell on it and never to mention it in front of Hannah. Hannah already felt bad enough about everything without her piling on other drama.

Beside her laptop, her cell phone vibrated. It was Jared, and that brought a real smile to her face.

Morning! I'm about to go to bed, but I wanted to wish you a good day.

It was times like this when she could believe that he did love her, that what they were building on was something as important to him as it was to her. She held these little moments close to her. It wasn't often that he thought to do the little things like this. He wasn't thoughtful in the way that Garrett was. There were no trinkets just because he was thinking about her. There were no surprise flower deliveries because he knew she liked them, but that was okay. That's who Jared was, and she could deal with that, but she wasn't sure she could deal with the lack of feeling.

Thanks! I hope you have a good day too!

Overuse of exclamation points, another thing that told her just how much she wanted this to work with him. She was willing to act like everything was fine, even be overly cheerful about it. That was not her at all. If he noticed, he didn't say anything about it, and that pissed her off too. All she wanted him to do was care about her the way she cared about him. Turning the phone over with more force than needed, she went back to the application, hoping that she was doing the right thing. As she read along with what she needed, there was a knock at the bus door.

Glancing out, she saw that they were stopped at a convenience store, and she wondered who in the world would be knocking. She got up and walked up to the front of the bus, her eyes widening when she saw Garrett standing outside.

"What are you doing here? I thought we were picking you up later on today?" she asked as she let him in.

"I texted the bus driver to see where you all were and it wasn't too far from the airport that I flew into. Since I knew he had to gas up and that would take a while, I decided it would be easier just to go ahead and meet you all. Is she still asleep?" he asked as he made his way onto the bus and sat his bag down.

"Yeah, I didn't want to wake her up, she's been so tired lately with everything going on."

Garrett shrugged out of his hoodie and sat it down on top of his bag. "I don't blame you; she seems very stressed when I've talked to her on the phone the last few times. I hate what this is doing to her, and then all that bullshit with Bryson? I have half a mind to find that fucker myself."

"I'm always up for assholes getting what they deserve, and I think he deserves whatever you give him. There was no reason for him to bring Hannah into that, unless of course what she said was true. The record company made promises on her behalf that she never intended to keep."

He nodded, but even then, Garrett didn't think it mattered. He didn't trust the fucker, and that was all there was to it. "I'm gonna head on back if that's okay with you."

"Sure." She smiled softly. "Go see your wife. She's missed you."

"Oh, before I forget." He reached into the pocket of the hoodie he had just taken off and pulled out an envelope. "Jared told me to give this to you."

For a long time, Shell held it in her hands, not sure what to do with it. Did she open it? What if it was a 'see ya later' letter? Finally, after glancing up at the clock and realizing that she'd held the envelope for over an hour, she steeled herself and tore into it. If he wanted to be alone, she had to know; there was no point in following along with Hannah when Black Friday toured next year, if that was the case.

Shell,

I know I try your patience, I know that I'm not the type of man that you thought you'd end up with, and I know that you're a saint for putting up with me. I don't tell you half the things you deserve to know or half the things I think about you. I was at Garrett's the other night and overheard something that Hannah was talking to him about. You confessed that I'd never told you I loved you, and Hannah was all over Garrett's shit for it.

She's a great friend, one you need to keep for the rest of your life.

Hearing her say the things she did made me feel like a piece of shit, and maybe that's what I needed. I've taken you for granted for a long time, beautiful, because you've been here, and I always assumed you would be. From the moment we had coffee with each other, I always knew you would be in my life, I never thought of it another way. It's my fault that you don't know how I feel about you because I can't put those feelings into words. That's why I'm writing this right now, I can't open my mouth and tell you these things.

My childhood was not a good one, and I never knew what the word love meant until I was a teenager. I love Garrett, he's my best friend. I love the guys, they've had my back forever, they've seen me do things that should have disgusted them, but instead they've always picked me up when I fall. I love the Thompson's, without them, I wouldn't be who I am today. I would be thirty-thousand times more fucked up and on the streets with a needle in my arm.

But you, you…you've taught me a different kind of love. One that I never hoped I would know. I didn't dare, because I knew I wasn't worthy and I knew that I wasn't capable. Michelle, you blew that notion, that assumption, out of the water. It was gradual and it took me a while to realize what the catch in my breath, the double beat of my heart was whenever I saw you, but never doubt it's not felt. Never doubt that it's not there. I may not be conventional, and I may not be able to tell you the words in person yet—I'm working on it. I will always be a work in progress, and I need you to understand that.

I love you. I love everything about you.

I'm so sorry you wondered, because there should not be one sliver of doubt in your mind.

Jared

It was hard to see through the tears that clouded her eyes, and it was even harder to swallow past the tightness in her throat, but she did it. Shell picked up the phone and placed the most important call of her life, and when he picked up, she knew that everything wouldn't be perfect all the time, but she knew that with him she could handle it. As long as he loved her, she could do anything in the world.

Chapter Twenty-Five

G arrett didn't know what was in the letter he'd handed Shell, and he didn't wait around to find out. That was between her and Jared. He'd done what he could in trying to convince Jared that he needed to let the woman in his life know exactly what she meant to him. Other than that, he was staying out of it. Jared was the type of man to do what he wanted to do, and Garrett knew that. He only hoped he'd done what he should have.

Quietly, he made his way into Hannah's room and shut the door. It was still very early in the morning; he'd flown all night but had managed to get some sleep on the plane. There was nothing he enjoyed more than to wrap up with her, though, so he was going to take complete advantage of the situation. He'd purposely packed a bunch of DVDs and some snacks in the bag he'd left out in the lounge area. They were going to relax if it killed them. They didn't do much of it, always on the go, always trying to fit in this and that. He was going to lie down with her and make sure she rested, no matter how bored he got.

Taking off everything but his boxer briefs, he quickly got under the covers and pulled her to him. A sigh of contentment escaped him when Hannah molded her body to his and clasped his hand in her sleep. He couldn't wait when this was where they would both be for longer than a few nights here and there. He rested better with her around; he felt more at peace and more at ease when she was around. Garrett wouldn't admit it to anyone, but he needed this—this grounded him in ways that other things never had. Without her, he could feel himself slipping into bad habits. He was drinking too much, and when that happened, he was an asshole. The relief of knowing that they only had a week of this left was astounding. Curling his arm around her head, he got as close as he could and inhaled the smell that was Hannah. His mind, heart, and soul finally at peace, he drifted off.

Hannah inhaled deeply, stretching against the sheets on her bed. Something was different from when she'd gone to sleep. It was warmer and she felt safe. Glancing down, she saw tattoos and a strong forearm around her waist. Sometime while she slept, Garrett had come in. With a smile stretching across her face, she ran her fingers over his forearm, tracing some of the ink there. She would never get over how much she loved that about him. Behind her, he jerked at her touch.

"Han?" His voice was deep with sleep, her favorite way.

"Yeah." She rolled over in his arms so that she could

see his face. "When did you get here?" she asked, reaching up to place a kiss on his jawline. It wasn't smooth, so she knew he hadn't been there long enough to shave.

"Early this morning. Shell let me in. Everything just happened to work out right, and I was able to meet the bus," he explained, running a hand over his face to try and help him wake up.

"I'm glad you're here." She squeezed his hip and pushed her way closer to him.

He smiled against her hair, closing his eyes against the sunlight that was coming in between her blinds. "I was hoping to surprise you. I didn't expect to fall asleep, but I guess I needed it more than I thought."

She had the feeling that he didn't sleep any better than she did when they were apart. This was taking a toll on the both of them, and she would be glad when it was done. They both needed a break. Hannah ran her hands up his stomach and chest before clasping her hands around his neck, burrowing her face into the space where his shoulder allowed her to fit perfectly. "You probably did. This hasn't been hard on only me. I'm glad you were able to rest. What time is it?"

He turned so that he could see the clock and laughed. "Almost one in the afternoon. Damn."

"Good thing this is a travel day, huh?"

"Well I had planned to keep you in bed all day anyway," he threw out off-handedly. "Not like that," he laughed when she smirked at him. "I brought a ton of DVDs, and I loaded my iPad with games. We are relaxing today."

"Sex is relaxing," she whispered against his ear,

snaking her tongue out to try and tempt him.

"No, we always do that when we're alone together." He pushed her away. "And then you go away or I go away, and it sucks. We have a week left, we can last. We're watching movies and playing games today."

She pursed her lips and removed her hands from around his neck "If you say so."

"I do."

He was so adamant about it that she couldn't help but laugh. "Fine, so do tell, what are we going to do first?"

"First," he said as he got up and swung his legs over the bed. "You need to eat, so I'm going to go find us something and check on Shell."

"Wait." She sat up, surprise in her voice. "Why are you checking on Shell? Did something happen while I was asleep?"

"Jared gave me a letter to give to her."

Fear gripped her heart. "It wasn't a break-up letter was it?" she blurted out before she could stop herself.

"I don't know, Hannah," he told her as patiently as possible. "I didn't read it before I gave it to her, and I didn't stick around once I did give it to her. I wanted to give her some privacy, just in case it was bad, but I think it was okay. Jared and I had a talk before I left to come here. I think I explained to him what she needed to hear if he does in fact feel that way about her. He asked me to give it to her. I've done that, now I want to make sure she's okay."

He was such a good guy, such a good friend. He would do anything for anyone that asked him. It was one of the things she loved most about him. "If she needs me, will you please let me know?"

"I will," he told her as he put his clothes back on. "I have to see this through, though. I brought it to her; I want to make sure she's okay."

Hannah stood up from the bed and walked over to where he stood. She carefully twined her arms around his neck and pulled him down so that she could brush her lips over his. "I know, and I love you for it."

That wasn't exactly what he was going for, but Garrett knew he would take it, no matter what. "Be right back."

It was hard for her to let him go in the other room and try to take care of her friend. It went against everything that she and Shell had stood for in their relationship, but she had to acknowledge that maybe that was a part of growing up too. Maybe Garrett could now give Shell what she never could—a glimpse into what it was like to be with Jared and understand him. She had to let them do this—not only for them, but for herself too. She had to trust that Garret knew what he was doing, and she had to trust that Shell would be okay if good news or bad news didn't come from her.

"Hey," Garrett started as he walked into the sitting area. Shell still sat in front of her laptop but looked up when he made his presence known. He watched her for signs of distress just like he would Hannah. Relieved, he saw that there were no red eyes, no puffy skin, and no tear tracks. "You okay?"

Shell chuckled. "If you're trying to ask me if Jared

broke up with me, the answer is no. He told me a lot of things in that letter that I needed to hear, and I'm thankful that you brought it to me."

"Thank God," he breathed deeply, running his hands through his hair. "I'm not going to lie. I was nervous."

"How the hell do you think I felt when you gave it to me?"

He turned to the fridge and began rummaging around in it. "Well, at least now this doesn't have to be all awkward. I told Hannah to let me come out here and talk to you about it because I felt like I had to. Really, though, I was afraid you were going to bust me in the balls if he'd broken up with you. You know, shooting the messenger and all that." He spared a glance back at her.

"No." She winked. "You're safe." She watched him for a few more minutes as he continued to make a huge amount of noise going through the fridge. "Garrett, what in the fuck are you looking for?"

"Some food, woman. What the hell do the two of you eat?"

She snorted at his frustration. "Normally we are stocked up, but the tour ends in a week. Neither one of us is thinking about food. If you want, I can get the bus to stop, run out, and grab all of us something."

"That would be awesome, I'm starving."

Garrett called Hannah into the main room, and they looked up the closest fast food restaurants to where they were. Within minutes, Shell had a list and they were stopping in the parking lot.

"Don't forget my honey mustard," Hannah yelled as

Shell went to leave.

"For the hundredth time in five minutes, I will get your damn honey mustard."

Hannah giggled as Shell made her way off the bus. "I love to make her mad. She's so easy to rile up, but I'm glad to see that whatever was in that letter from Jared wasn't bad. The one thing about Shell is that she can't hide what she's feeling. If it was bad, we would know. She even seems at peace."

"I would agree with that," Garrett told her as he grabbed his bag and pulled a DVD out of it.

"Do I even get a say-so in what movie we watch?"

"No, I came to you, and this time we do what I say."

She wasn't sure if she liked that at all, but there was something very cute about him being bossy this way. "Fine," she sighed. "Can we watch it out here, at least? I don't want Shell to be lonely."

That was a concession that he was willing to make. Within minutes, Shell had brought their food back, and all of them were situated in the back lounge. Garrett and Hannah snuggled together on the couch; Shell lay out in the recliner. Garrett would never tell anyone this out loud, but it was the most relaxed he'd been in weeks. Here, in a dark lounge in the back of a bus, his wife snuggled to his chest eating chicken strips, a horrible action-adventure movie playing, and her best friend sitting to the side doing the same thing as the two of them. This was a huge departure from years past, but he knew with everything that he was, he would not change this for anything. If there was one thing that Hannah had brought to his life, it was stability, and he no longer had to be the life of the party. This was now the party, and he had never been happier. Leaning down, he brushed a kiss against her forehead. This was where he saw himself in five years, and he hoped with everything he had that she was with him all the time. It was selfish, but it was the truth.

Chapter Twenty-Six

Hannah had expected the days since Garrett's departure to drag, but that hadn't been the case. It was as if one day she woke up and realized that this was it. They'd made it to the end of the tour. Only one more show stood in their way, and then she could be Hannah Thompson. She could be the person that she'd been longing to be for what seemed like forever. Of course, she knew that was an exaggeration, but she was okay with that.

"When's Garrett going to be here?" Shell asked as they moved around the bus, packing up last-minute essentials.

Hannah stole a glance at her phone. "He should be landing right now. He and Jared were going to rent a car, I think, because Garrett and I are doing the four-hour drive to Nashville tomorrow. We want to check on the house that's finally ours and figure out what we want to do for the holiday." Thanksgiving was in a week, and they still had yet to decide which family and which coast they would be spending it on. It was something that Hannah hadn't wanted to mess with on top of everything else that was already going on. She was fine with letting it play out however it would. Tomorrow she would start worrying all about that.

"Good, because I'm flying back with Jared, but if you have a car, then that means you can take most of my luggage to the house?"

"Sure, just let me know which suitcases you want taken over there, and I'll be glad to do it."

They busied themselves with getting the rest of what they needed off the bus, and suddenly, it came to a stop.

"We're here," Shell told her quietly.

Here was the Phillips Arena.

Hannah glanced out the window to the place they had been waiting for since this whole thing began. It seemed like both a lifetime ago and only yesterday that she had taken a look at the grueling touring schedule they'd placed in front of her. There had been times when she wondered if she could do it. There were other times when she wondered if she wanted to do it. She remembered with startling clarity the nights that she'd cried herself to sleep because she'd missed Garrett so much. On the other hand, she remembered all the amazing days off she had with him. Not being on tour would change the whole dynamic of her relationship with him, because more than likely in a few short months, he would be the one going on tour and she wouldn't be staying behind. This time she would be following along. It was an unknown for her, so it was scary, but at the same time, she was more than excited to being this next chapter.

"Let's go get ready for the show." She smiled, reaching over to give Shell a hug. "My makeup ain't gonna do itself."

"Is it weird to feel like I'm walking into the unknown and scared shitless?" Shell asked her as they made their way off the bus, both holding what was left of their bags.

"No." She shook her head. "I feel the same way too. Neither one of us have ever had this much time coming to us. We've never had the option. I feel like we're seniors and we're graduating from high school, ready to take college by storm but wanting so badly to stay at home and be the children we've always been."

"The irony of that statement is that we both went from being seniors in high school to doing this," Shell laughed.

That was the irony. Ever since they had been adults, neither one of them had what anyone would call a normal life.

"Guess we better get ready for the freshman fifteen then," Hannah joked as they made their way into the back of the arena.

Just in case this was the last time she did this, Hannah took a moment to glance behind her. She took note of the setting sun behind her tour bus, the hustle and bustle of everyone getting the equipment ready for the show. She took a minute to look around the side. From where she stood, she could see the line of people coming to see her already forming. Tears gathered in her eyes and she breathed deeply. The journey she was about to embark on was the most important of her life, but if anyone asked her, she would tell them that she had never been so scared. Ever.

"You coming?" Shell asked, holding her hand out for her friend.

"Yeah."

"Wanted to remember it, huh?"

Hannah nodded. She wasn't sure that she could push the words past the tightening in her throat. "I do, just in case I don't come back."

Shell pulled her into a tight hug. "You know that whatever you decide I'm a hundred percent behind you."

"Are you sure? You were pretty ticked at me when I started talking about this."

"That was me being an idiot, and I am sorry for ever putting you through that. That was my own insecurities. You are always going to be the best friend I've ever had, just like you tell me. Whether you come back to this or not, we will always be close. I promise you that."

That was exactly what Hannah had needed to hear. The two of them made their way through the back halls and into the dressing room. Hannah took a deep breath, sat down at the makeup table, and went about putting on her face. This was the face that many fans would have to remember for a long time to come.

"Atlanta! I want to thank you from the bottom of my heart for coming out tonight," she spoke clearly into the mic, trying to keep her voice from cracking. "As many of you know, this is my last show for a while."

The announcement was met with a huge round of applause. "I hope you're clapping because you're happy about what I'm going to be doing," she laughed as she looked over to the side of the stage where Garrett stood. "I'll be spending all kinds of time with my husband." More loud cheering and screaming. "But before we go into the last two songs of the night, I want to say thank you for all the support. I want to tell you how excited I am that you've accepted me and Reaper into your lives. Our song, which is sitting at number freakin' two right now, means a lot to us, and I hope it means just as much to you." She stopped, gathering her breath and courage. "Having said that, I'm going to invite Reaper out to sing it with me—you know, if that's okay with you?"

The response was so great she could feel it in her chest. The screams and stomps of feet reverberated in her body. It got even louder as Garrett made his way onto the stage. "Thanks for coming," she told him as he leaned down, kissing her on the cheek.

He had to yell to be heard. "Wouldn't miss it for anything. To be honest, I'd hoped you would ask me out here to do this song."

One of the stage hands brought two stools out, and they had a seat facing each other. "Say hi," she told Garrett as she indicated the crowd. He waved, smiling over at her. "I hope we aren't giving you a bad reputation. You're charting on a country chart, and now I've pulled you out to sing at a country show for the second time."

He glanced over at her. "I'll do anything you ask me to, babe." That was met with the cooing of the entire crowd, and he flashed them a thumbs-up.

"Since we're pretty much re-enacting the way we did this in the hotel room that we shot the YouTube video in, I'd like to invite my friend Shell and Black Friday's lead guitarist Train."

The two of them were also met with a thunderous applause. As the foursome got situated and Jared made sure the guitar was in tune, Hannah took another moment for reflection. She'd caught herself doing that many times as the night and concert had progressed. She wanted to make sure she remembered each moment as she went through it; she wanted to remember exactly how she felt. It was no longer the best feeling in the world to her, but she wanted to make sure that she was completely in this experience.

"You ready?" Garrett asked, his deep voice echoing through the arena.

"If you are."

"Always ready when it comes to you, babe," he told her, leaning over to place a soft kiss on her cheek.

The song they sung was about loving each other regardless of the imperfections they both had. It was about loving someone when all the obstacles stood in the way. Somehow, here, in front of this arena full of people, it felt even more intimate than it had in the hotel room. Garrett would not move his eyes from her as he sang, and she found herself having to look away, the emotion too much for her. He brought her right back to him every time she looked away. By the time they were done, there were cell phones up in every part of the arena, she had tears streaming down her face, and he'd stood up to hold her next to his side.

"Thanks for letting me come hang out with you tonight, Atlanta! I appreciate it," he told them before kissing her again and making his way off the stage. The songs that would follow and the little amount of time they had left in the concert would be hers. He would never steal anything like that from her or her fans. He watched her turn her back to the crowd and seem to collect herself. "C'mon, babe, you got this," he yelled from where he stood, clapping his hands for her.

Her brown eyes glanced over and met his, offering him a small smile. She nodded and exhaled before turning back around. Harmony was back on and would be for as long as Hannah needed her to be.

"You okay?" Garrett asked two hours later as he helped her drag her suitcases to the car. He stole a glance at her. The stage makeup was gone, her hair was in a top knot on her head, and she had on sweatpants and a hoodie. She looked like she was student moving into the dorms on her first day of college. She had been quiet, and he couldn't help but worry about her.

"I'm good." Her smile was shaky, but it was there. "I'm just a little emotional and I'm tired. I think after I get a good night's sleep I'll be okay."

"Not regretting it, are you?" That was a big fear of his, and he was afraid she would regret it as soon as he walked off the stage for the final time.

"Never. I have the most peaceful feeling in the world surrounding me right now. I'm a little raw though, I need some time to decompress. The past year has been insane, and honestly we're lucky the past few months didn't drive me to a nervous breakdown. I'll be fine; I just need a few days."

He stopped what he was doing and walked over, scooping her up in his arms. He hugged her for a long time before kissing her tenderly. "I love you and I thank you for the sacrifices you've made for us."

"They aren't any different than yours. We love each other, and as long as we remember that, we'll be good."

As they got into the car and began the drive north, he still hoped against all he had that she would not come to regret the decisions that she had made.

Chapter Twenty-Seven

Just as Garrett had figured, as soon as they were an hour outside of Atlanta and well after midnight, Hannah fell asleep in the passenger seat beside him. Taking his eyes off the road for a second, he glanced over at her and realized that his heart was full. She was his for longer than she'd been his in the entire time they'd been together. He had so many things he wanted to do with her, so many things he wanted to show her. Truth be told, he was tired too. He was tired of the distance, of the separation, and of pretending like it didn't matter so much to him. When he didn't show it, it didn't seem to wear on her as much, but there was only so much he could take. He was at the end of that rope with it all. He was ready to have his wife with him, and to know that they would soon be celebrating the holidays together was one of the most exciting feelings he'd ever had.

Reaching over, he clasped her hand in his and squeezed tightly. The first order of business would be to get some weight back on her and remove the dark circles from under her eyes. The tiredness he'd seen there lately he didn't like one bit. The way her smile didn't touch her eyes, the beaten-down look. That needed to be gone. Garrett was ready for a bit of normalcy with them, even though he knew he'd soon be dragging her out on his tour, it would be easier with the two of them in the same spot for more than a couple of days.

Hours later, he pulled into the driveway of his in-laws and carefully got out of the car, keeping it running so that he wouldn't wake Hannah up. Robert met him on the front porch, surprising Garrett. He said so, asking what the older man was doing awake.

"I was watching for you," he explained. "Do you need some coffee or anything? I know you've driven all night."

Garrett shook his head. "Nah, I'm good."

Robert reached into his pocket and pulled out the keys to the house that he'd been taking care of for them. "We got some groceries for you yesterday. I had some of the guys from my shop help me move in a little bit of furniture. I figure if you don't like it, you can use it in the studio. Just a couch, a chair, a TV, and a Blu-Ray player. The bed you ordered was delivered yesterday too, and Liz made sure there are sheets and stuff on it. Heat's on and it should be ready for the two of you."

"Thank you so much, you have no idea how much we appreciate this." Garrett reached out, shaking Robert's hand.

"Just take care of her. She's had a rough couple of years."

Garrett looked back at the car, knowing that Hannah slept peacefully inside. "She is my number-one priority."

"That's what I wanted to hear. Please let us know

what you two want to do for Thanksgiving."

Garrett had almost forgotten that it was so close, even though he'd been thinking about the holidays on the drive up. "As soon as we get settled, that will be the first thing we talk about." It was then that a jaw-popping yawn made its way out of his mouth.

"Go, get some sleep. Call us if you need anything, and we'll figure everything out in the next few days."

Garrett surprised himself by reaching over and hugging the other man. He felt closer to Robert than he expected to feel, and he figured that was a part of the growing-up process, a part of welcoming more people into his family. Quickly, he made his way back to the car.

It was a good thing they had a GPS, because if asked, Garrett wouldn't be able to tell anyone how they had gotten to their new home. It had been a maze of turns, and he wanted only one thing—to get home. Home sounded like such a good word. He couldn't wait to make this home with her. It had been one of the only things that had kept him going through their long separation.

He pulled into the garage and shut the door before turning the car off. "Han." He reached over and gently shook her shoulder. When it was obvious she wasn't going to wake up, he unbuckled and went over to the passenger side. Carefully, he got her out and let them both inside. He hoped like hell he remembered which room the two of them had decided on. A pang of loneliness hit him too when he didn't hear the clickety-clack of Havock's toenails against the floor. They would have to bring their boy out here; as it was, Garrett hated leaving him.

The stairs weren't easy with her limp in his arms, but he navigated them. When he got to their room, he breathed a sigh of relief. The freshly made bed looked like an oasis in the middle of a desert. He was running on fumes, and he knew she was too. There wasn't anything left in either of them. He moved back the cover as best he could with one hand and laid her down; he then lay down next to her, still fully clothed. He pulled the cover up around them. That would have to be enough. The exhaustion of the last few months weighed on him, and he finally let it go, closing his eyes, putting his arms around Hannah, and letting it all go.

Hannah felt like she was some place she'd been before, but she couldn't place it. She knew that Garrett was with her because she could feel his body behind hers. Prying her eyes open, she looked around. They were in their new house and it was dusk outside. How long had they been here? Pulling her cell phone out of her pocket, she saw that it was four o'clock in the evening. The last thing she remembered was getting in the car a little after midnight that morning. Had she really slept for over twelve hours?

"Garrett." She nudged his shoulder.

His eyes popped open and he glanced at her. "Yeah?"

"It's four thirty at night. Have we slept that long?"

He sat up, wiping the sleep from his face and eyes. "Damn," he mumbled, pulling his own cell phone out of his pocket. She was right, it was four and they had been there all day. "Yeah, we have," he laughed, running a hand through his hair. "I guess we needed it."

She lay back against the sheet and breathed deeply. She had no place to be, she had nothing to do. There wasn't another concert that she had to rush to; there was no interview to prep for. Her schedule was as clear as the window to her right. The feeling was odd, one that she'd never had before. For some reason, she started to giggle.

"Are you okay?" he asked, staring over at her, a smile on his face.

"Yes," she laughed. "I don't know why I'm laughing, but I have a free schedule. Do you know how good that feels? I don't have to be anywhere at any certain time, I don't have to clear my schedule with anyone, and I can be with you whenever I want."

He answered her laugh with a deep exhale of his own. "It does feel fuckin' good, but you know what would feel really good right now?"

She shook her head, not sure where he was going with this.

"A shower and some food. I feel nasty and I'm about to starve."

"We're not showering together," she told him as she swung her legs over the side of the bed. "I remember what happened last time we did that."

He gave her a slow smile. "We don't have enough time for that right now. My stomach's about to eat itself, and I wouldn't be able to give you my full attention. Now, after I get the shower and some food in me, I wouldn't mind getting in you."

She shook her head at him. "Couldn't help it, could ya?"

"Nope."

Hannah watched as he made his way out of the bedroom, hoping they had towels and changes of clothes somewhere. If not, there was going to be a lot of naked lounging in this family. Standing up, she stretched, sighing as her back and neck cracked. The tension she'd carried for so long was gone. She felt like she could breathe, and it had been a very long time since she had felt that way. The intense pressure that she'd been under for the last few months was gone. It felt amazing. She felt lighter as she made her way down the stairs and into the foyer. With no suitcases to be found, she guessed they were still in the car. They would need them, and she had been self-sufficient for most of her life when it came to her own luggage.

Walking out into the garage, she saw that she was right. This wasn't the first time she'd had to lug her bags, and she knew that it wouldn't be the last. They were just a lot heavier than she remembered. After minutes of struggling, she had both one of hers and one of Garrett's in the foyer.

"Han?"

"Right here," she told him, breathing hard.

"Babe, I would have grabbed that stuff."

She looked up, laughing as he held a small towel around his waist. She wasn't even sure it went completely around his waist. "Where did you find that?"

"The kitchen." He shrugged. "I had to have something."

"That's why I grabbed these; I had some towels in my bag." She giggled as he turned around, showing her his exposed butt cheeks.

"Now you tell me."

She snorted. "You never asked. It was all 'I'm gonna take a shower, get some food, and then...'"

"Please say it," he whispered. Amusement made the edges of his mouth twitch. "Please say it."

Hannah couldn't bring herself to say it. "You know what you said."

"I do know what I said," he told her, pulling her close to him.

They were so close that she could feel the moisture of the shower he'd just taken. Hannah needed to feel a part of him. She wrapped her arms around his waist and tilted her face up to his. The invitation was clear, and Garrett didn't make her wait long. Like he always did, he possessed her with one of the hottest kisses she'd ever had in her life, and that was saying something, given their history.

His stomach picked that moment to growl loudly. "Can we come back to this?" he asked, rubbing a hand over the skin there.

"Yeah." She shook her head, laughing quietly. "We can, because I really need that shower."

"I'll cook," he offered, bending over in front of her. "Don't you dare smack my ass either," he threw over his shoulder at her.

"Wouldn't dream of it," she told him as she smacked him quickly and then made a run for the stairs.

"You're lucky that I'm hungry."

Feeling a bit ornery, she put an extra sway into her hips as she climbed the stairs. "Promises, promises."

He watched her, an evil glint in his eye. She would find out about those promises.

Chapter Twenty-Eight

"I'm lucky that you're not only hot, but you cook pretty well too." Hannah smiled at Garrett over their dinner.

They had set up camp in the living room, both sitting on the couch with the TV on some horrible reality TV show. They both had beers, and he'd whipped them up a couple of grilled cheese sandwiches a piece. They had found a bag of chips, and they'd dove into that like they hadn't eaten in days. He put half of the sandwich in his mouth and chewed thoroughly before taking a healthy drink of the beer. "I told you, there are certain things you learn to do as a bachelor. Omelets and grilled cheeses are number one and number two on the list."

She picked up half of the sandwich he'd made her and took a bite. The food tasted better when it was shared with him, it felt like it satisfied a hunger in her. Just by being together, she was more at peace. Her stomach no longer had the queasy feeling she'd had the entire time she'd been on the road. In hindsight, she wasn't even sure that she'd known it was there, but now—now she knew how stressed she had been.

"Thanks for cooking me dinner."

"Anything for you," he told her, swiping a chip off her plate.

She swatted at his hand, but in reality she couldn't help but notice how at ease he appeared to be too. There was no tension at the side of his eyes, he looked semi-well rested, and the smile was much easier to come to his face when he looked at her. Sighing, she moved her plate and his before throwing herself into his arms.

"What's that for?" he asked, rubbing his hand up and down her back.

"Because I can and because I love you."

This was what had been missing between the two of them. Meeting in hotel rooms made it feel like their love was illicit, and while that was fun sometimes, nobody liked to feel like they weren't supposed to be together. He wanted to show her exactly what he was capable of. That he wanted this. He wanted to make it all work and he'd been waiting on it. He'd told her that it didn't matter how long it would take, he would wait, and he had. Now was the time to put up or shut up. She would need him just as much here as she needed him while she was on tour. Now was the time for him to prove how serious he was and how in the marriage he wanted to be. If he didn't start this minute, this second, then what kind of a man was he? "You wanna go sit on the wraparound porch?"

Her eyes moved over to the French doors, eyeing the frost on them. "Isn't it cold?"

"We can take a blanket and huddle together."

That suggestion sounded awesome to her. She loved sitting near him and letting his body heat warm her. He was like her own personal furnace most of the time. "Okay, let's go." She got up from the couch and grabbed the two blankets that someone had left there for them. During the day, Nashville wasn't too bad, but at night, it got cooler—definitely cooler than what Garrett was used to.

They walked out, both pleased to discover the lounger used to help stage the home was still there. Garrett had a seat on it and then pulled Hannah into his arms so that her back pressed against his front. They quickly covered themselves up with both blankets to ward off the cold.

"Maybe I should have worn a sweatshirt instead of a T-shirt," she laughed, her teeth chattering against the cold.

Garrett ran his hands up and down her arms, trying to keep her as warm as possible. "Do you think it'll be colder next week?" he asked, blowing out a breath to see it show white against the cold.

"Hard to say," she shrugged. "Thanksgiving is iffy sometimes. Speaking of, do we want to have it here or not?"

It surprised him to admit it, but he did. "I do, I would love for everyone to get together in our new house. Do you think the west coast family would be up for it?"

She turned in his arms. "Garrett, the question is, are we up for it? We have nothing in this house except for a couch, a chair, and a bed. Do you think we could pull it together?"

"I think so. I mean, all we really need is furniture. I'm sure between the two of us we have enough *fame*," he snickered at his own joke, "to get furniture in here. I'm sure our moms would love to cook in our new house."

"Can we get Havock out here?"

"Definitely, I miss the dude."

"Me too." She smiled up at him, impulsively leaning up to place a kiss on his lips.

What started out as an innocent expression of happiness quickly heated up between the two of them. His large hands settled around her hips, adjusting her to the way he wanted her, his tongue coaxed hers out to play with his.

"Garrett," she moaned, twining her arms around his neck and settling herself more fully against him. "We're outside."

"And there's no one around," he whispered against her lips. "That's the awesome thing about this place; there is no one who could see back here for miles." He gestured out to the woods that butted up to the back of the property. There were neighbors on either side of them, but none could see in the back of the house. "C'mon, babe, we have to christen our new house."

"The house," she laughed. "Not the back porch."

"It's an extension." He ignored her protests, moving one hand up to curl around her neck. He'd learned in the time they'd been together that was her spot; she loved when he did anything with her neck. Lightly, he massaged the muscles there, no longer tense with the strain of separation. She was putty in his arms as he used his thighs to separate hers.

"I'm serious," she protested.

He knew he had her when her neck tilted back, allowing his mouth to claim the soft skin there.

"Shit," she whispered, giggling as she did so. "You make me do all the things I said I would never do."

"Baby, I will gladly be your bad influence forever." His fingers played with the hem of her T-shirt, pushing his hands up the back.

"So warm," she breathed, arching into the strength of his hands. Her body began a slow grind against his, and she knew she was done for.

Moving his hands from her back, he cupped her chest through her T-shirt, not willing to take it off. It was cold and he didn't want her to get sick, but that didn't mean they couldn't have a little fun first. Molding his hands against the front of her shirt, he saw just how cold it was. The way she grasped his hair as he moved his head down and stuck his tongue against the pebbled flesh there enflamed him. His lips teased, and his hands moved in opposite directions, one grasping her hip, showing her the way he wanted her to move, the other tangling in her hair.

Hannah dared a glance down at him and moaned loudly. It was dark, but she could make out the edges of his lashes against his skin. His eyes fluttered lazily as he continued to work her skin between his lips. Needing to feel him the way he was feeling her, she unhooked her arms from around his neck and let them travel down the length of his chest and stomach. Once there she pushed up against the fabric but didn't take it off. Her hands stroked the ink on his abdominal muscles before slipping past the edge of the sweat pants he wore.

"You sure you wanna do that?" he asked, letting her go for a half a second.

She moaned, nodding her head as he went back to work on her. Pushing his sweat pants further down his hips, she felt the hard length of him against her hand as she groped him in the dark.

In response, he hooked his thumbs in her own sweats and pulled harshly down on them.

She wasn't sure how they managed it, but she got hers off and he got his down around his knees. It was just enough room for them to work with one another. Hannah sank down on him, sighing deeply in her throat.

"Every time, I wonder if this will be the time that you don't blow my mind," he confessed, caressing her stomach and helping her pump up and down against him.

"Surprised you, huh?"

Her voice was strained and damn near the most erotic thing he'd ever heard in his life. "You did, but I've never been happier for a surprise in my life. I was meant to find you, and I thank God every day that I did."

She felt the same way, and there was no one who would ever be able to tell her different. After Ashton, she'd truly given up and thought that maybe love wasn't in the cards for her. Maybe she was supposed to be an entertainer and make people happy that way. Meeting and falling in love with Garrett had been so far off her radar that she was pretty sure that no one was more surprised than her. If someone had told her this was where she'd be a year ago, she would have told them to go get their head's checked. "Agreed."

Like it tended to do between the two of them, the feelings and the chemistry took over. The only sounds were the sounds of nature and their bodies grinding against one another. Garrett moved his hand to her neck and then up, cupping her cheek. Using his thumb, he rubbed the pad of it against her lip. It was the biggest turn on of his life when she clamped it between her white teeth and nipped at the flesh there.

"Use your tongue to soothe the bite," he told her, barely hanging on. This woman did it for him, in the biggest way. If anyone asked him to pinpoint it, he wouldn't be able to, it was everything about Hannah.

She did as she was told. It excited her, to be able to surprise him, to do something that would take her out of her comfort zone. They had a lot of time to make up for, and she knew she was going to love making up that time with her husband.

With the thumb she'd just bitten and licked, he moved his hand down to the middle of her body where they were joined and pressed against the most sensitive part of her. Something about that gesture slammed through her and made her body clench.

"Fuck, Han" he ground out against her.

His lips were everywhere, and she gave up trying to follow them; her body clenching had made her hungry for more. She wanted what it seemed like only he could give her. "I know," she told him, grasping his hair in her fingers and tugging hard.

It was that touch of dominance that she exerted that set him off, which in turn set her off. As always, neither one of them knew where they were for a few moments afterwards.

"Did you really cuss?" he asked, his face a mask of shock.

"I think I did," she talked against his neck, where she

had collapsed. "In fact, I know I did. I didn't mean to, 'cause you know I think it's crass. But sometimes, with you, I wish I could say all the things I think."

"Oh baby, me too. One day I will make you tell me exactly what goes on in that head of yours."

She stayed quiet against his neck, smiling slightly. Those thoughts were her secrets and her secrets alone.

Chapter Twenty-Nine

Going shopping anywhere, including the pet store, two days before Thanksgiving was probably not the best idea that Garrett had ever had. It was beyond stressful, but at least in Nashville people didn't bother him. Not to mention he was very happy for the reason that he was at the pet store. His family should have arrived at Nashville International Airport a half hour ago, and they were bringing Havock along with them. He and Hannah had decided to divide and conquer—which meant she was at the airport and he was at the pet store.

His patience was beginning to wear thin with the line in front of him, but he needed everything that his cart was loaded down with. By some holiday miracle, their house was furnished—in a way they both liked—and was waiting on their family. The one thing they had forgotten was stuff for the dog, and both of them had felt awful. In his hand, his cell vibrated. He unlocked the screen and opened the message from Hannah. It was a picture of her and Havock. The text below it read: "Got our boy!"

He loved that she loved the dog as much as he did. The dog loved her even more, and now that they were together their lives would be normal. They had their house, their dog, and a few more months before they would have to be out on the road. Black Friday's record had been turned in, and while the record company wasn't thrilled with what Garrett and the boys had done, they were willing to give them some leeway. Finally it was his turn in line, and he quickly put all the stuff up on counter and then paid for it before walking outside into the crisp night air to put it all in the Land Rover. It had been busy when he got to the store, and he'd had to park around the side of the building.

"Did you get a leash for your bitch?"

Garrett was for sure the person talking wasn't speaking to him, but he also knew that no one else was putting anything in their cars. He sighed, knowing he didn't want to look up, but he did anyway. Standing not too far away was Bryson Grant. "Come again? I don't think I heard you correctly."

Bryson sauntered up closer, watching as Garrett continued putting away his purchases. "I asked if you got a leash for your bitch."

He had a pretty good idea of what the young prick was talking about, but wanted to be sure. "My dog is male, dude."

"I was talking about your wife."

He tried, he really did. He tried to curb the anger that coursed through his veins. Garrett tried to harness and leash it, but Bryson's attitude straight up pissed him off. He shook his head and licked his lips. Slamming the back of the vehicle up, he turned around. "What the fuck did you just say to me?"

"You heard me. I know you're the reason that Hannah wouldn't record that song with me. That was going to break me into the mainstream and that's her fault."

Garrett couldn't believe that this guy was a friend of Hannah's. He couldn't believe he was sitting here listening to him spew this bullshit. "C'mon."

Bryson's eyes widened and he took a step back. "What?"

"You, you wanna talk like a big-ass man, then c'mon. I'll beat your ass like a big-ass man." He grabbed the back of Bryson's neck and pulled him back behind the building and quickly got in his face. "I don't know who the fuck you think you are or what your beef is with my wife, but I'm about to be all up in your business."

"Man, I didn't mean to..."

"You didn't mean to call my wife a bitch? You didn't mean to throw her under the bus and talk shit about me in the press? You didn't mean any of that?" Garrett asked, putting his head up against Bryson's ear. He didn't want people to hear what was being said if anyone was around.

"I didn't want to cause problems."

"You know what my problem is with you, mother-fucker? The fact that you like my wife, and I don't mean as a friend. I'm not a dumbass and I'm not blind. I can see just fucking fine. I see the way you look at her; I've heard the way you talk about her in the press. You might be hot for her, but let me tell ya something, she's not hot for you. She's got all the man she needs right here. If I ever hear about you talking shit about her again, if you check her out again, if you even breath inappropriately towards her, I will kick your ass from here to next week."

"I heard that about you."

Garrett didn't know if this guy was brave or just fucking stupid. "You doubt it?" he asked, grabbing Bryson by the collar and shoving him hard up against the wall.

"Talkin' is easy."

Garrett smiled, laughing. "You think I talk shit?"

"I've heard that you talk shit."

"Who'd you hear that from? Ashton Coleman? He was talking out the side of his mouth for a couple of weeks after I got through with him."

Bryson just couldn't keep his mouth shut. "Regardless of what you did to Ashton Coleman, you tell your wife that she owes me a number one hit."

That was it, Garrett was done. Done listening to him, done being nice and done with it all. It wasn't in him to let shit go—especially when someone was talking about his wife. "I gave you a chance," he said as he reared back and let his fists do the talking.

Bryson put up a small fight, but Garrett was faster, stronger, taller, and he flat out didn't like the guy. Three shots and Bryson was slumped against the wall. "Remember the next time you think I talk shit but don't follow through who was left lying in a parking lot. Do not ever come near my wife again or I will seriously fuck you up."

He was mad as he went back to the car, pissed that someone had pushed him that far. No matter how much he would fight for his wife, he did not appreciate people pushing him into a corner, one bit. "Fuck." He beat the steering wheel with the heel of his hand. How was he going to explain this to Hannah?

He pulled into the driveway, noticing the extra cars. The family was here, and he had busted knuckles and dried blood on his hand. Pulling his phone out of his pocket, he called Jared, knowing that he would have come with the family.

"Hey, dude, we're at the house, where are you? This house is amazing by the way."

"Thanks, I just rolled in and I need a favor. Come out and help me carry this stuff in and bring me something to wipe my hands off with."

Jared was quiet for a moment. "Okay."

"I'll explain in a minute."

Garrett parked and waited for Jared to come out into the garage. It took him a few minutes, but he finally made his way out, carrying a washrag.

"What the fuck happened?" he asked, glancing at Garrett's knuckles when he started to wash them off.

"My fist ran into Bryson Grant's face."

Jared whistled. "What did he say?" He knew that whatever it was, wasn't good. Garrett might like to fight, might even need to sometimes, but he never fought for no reason, and judging by the shape of his knuckles, Garrett had kicked some ass.

"He thought he was cute when he saw me loading the shit for Havock in the car. Asked me if I had to get a leash for my bitch," he breathed deeply. "At first I was willing to let it go, but I asked him if I'd heard him correctly, then gave him a shot to back out of it when I told him that my dog was male. He told me he meant my wife."

"Seriously? Fuck, I can't believe you didn't murder

him." If there was one thing that all of them had learned about Garrett over the last few months, it was that there was no messing around with Hannah, there was no talking about her, there was no questioning her place in Garrett's life. More than that, she was their friend too, and he kind of wanted to shove his own fist in Bryson's mouth.

"It was difficult, but I thought about all the people I had here waiting on me to get home. I don't think we'll be hearing anything else out of him for a while. Next time I'll shove his dick down his throat."

"Hey, babe, did you finally make it back?"

Garrett hurried and cleaned his hands faster when he heard Hannah. "Yeah, Jared's helping me grab the stuff. Had to get Havock everything."

Jared grabbed bags, leaving the crate for Garrett to grab. "I got this if you get that."

Garrett turned around and was startled as Hannah stood in front of him. "You okay? You were gone a long time, and I saw Jared bring a washrag out here."

He couldn't lie to her, they'd never been liars to each other, and he wouldn't start now, even if it made things easier. "Bryson and I had words, and then my fists did the talking."

Hannah swallowed hard against the lump in her throat. "You can't go around doing that."

"Oh, I can when he calls my wife a bitch." He slapped his hand against his thigh. "I could have kept that from you, but I don't want you to think this fucker is your friend and then let him talk shit behind your back. He isn't the guy that you used to know. He let the lure of a number one hit make him turn his back on you. He doesn't deserve your loyalty or your friendship."

That hurt. "I can't believe he would say that, but then again, I know that sometimes when you get into this business you want to be number one. He obviously wants something that he doesn't have and feels like I can give him. I'm sorry that someone told him that, but you and I both know that song was never going to be his."

"I know." He reached over and hugged her close. "I know that it sucks to hear that, but I wasn't about to let him talk about you. Words were exchanged and then fists flew. He got the worst end of the deal." He smiled at her.

"I have a feeling that's usually the way it goes with you." She smiled back up at him. "I love you, and I love that you stick up for me. I wish you didn't have to, because honestly Bryson should have come to me."

"The fucker better be glad he didn't."

She loved the look that flashed in his eyes. It was possessive and real, and it was the look he gave only to her. "I'm a lucky woman, and I appreciate what you do for me, but you and I both know that one of the things that I'm working on is standing up for myself."

He could understand where she was coming from, but he didn't trust Bryson. "Promise me you won't seek him out. He's pissed and I laid his ass out. There's no telling what he might do. I'm not saying he would physically hurt you, but I know words hurt you just as much. Let it alone, babe."

Hannah knew he was right. Squeezing him around the waist hard one last time, she let go. "C'mon, your family and our boy are here. Let's go spend some time with the people that matter."

That was the best idea he'd heard all night.

Chapter Thirty

Hannah groaned as the alarm went off beside her head. It read six in the morning. She slapped it off and rolled over, curling her lip up at Garrett, who slept peacefully beside her. This was the first Thanksgiving that she'd been home in years and the very first Thanksgiving that she'd offered to help her mom cook—hence the alarm at six a.m.

Carefully pushing the covers back, she quickly got out of bed, shivering as the early morning air hit her bare skin. More often than not, now that they were together full time, she woke up with no clothes on. Fumbling around in the dark, she finally found underclothes, a pair of sweat pants, and a T-shirt. She snuck into the bathroom, quietly shutting the door. With half-closed eyes, she went about her business and then brushed her teeth, washed her face off, and secured her long hair in a top-knot to keep it out of her face.

"Okay, Han, this is what being an adult and wife is all about," she sighed as she gave herself the pep talk. She hadn't seen six a.m. since she had been through with the tour, and it surprised her how quickly she had forgotten how much it sucked.

As she walked out of the room, she heard the jingle of Havock's collar. "You wanna come with me, boy?" she whispered. He followed her out and she shut the door behind her.

He stretched in front of her and then obediently stood next to her, waiting to see where she would go. "C'mon," she told him as she made her way down the stairs and towards the noise she already heard in the kitchen.

"Morning, ladies," she greeted. Already there was her mom and her mother-in-law standing by the counter, Stacey sitting at the kitchen table, her forehead against the wood surface, and Shell standing at the coffee pot.

Without asking, Shell passed her the cup she held in her hands. "It's yours."

"I don't know what I would do without you," she told her sincerely, taking a sip and letting the caffeine rush through her body.

"Be bitchy. You're lucky we understand each other," Shell joked as she moved to have a seat beside Stacey.

"Are you alive over there?" Hannah asked as she nudged her sister-in-law.

"Barely. Just barely."

Liz and Marie stood next to each other, laughing at the younger girls. "It will be okay that you ladies woke up early. You'll make it," Marie assured them.

Surprisingly, Hannah was excited. "What do we need to do?"

Liz walked over to her daughter and felt her forehead. "Are you sick? Because you're never this agreeable in the morning."

"It's all the sex she's getting."

Hannah spit her coffee out and threw the first thing she picked up at Shell's head. "Really?" Her face burned hot; she couldn't believe that Shell had said that in front of the older women. Didn't matter how old she was, it would always embarrass her.

"Oh c'mon," Shell argued. "You're a newlywed for God's sake."

"Still." She covered her cheek with her hand, feeling how hot it was.

"Trust me, Hannah." Marie winked. "I know my son is a good-looking man."

Dear God, could the floor not open up and swallow her right now. "I got nothin'," she said as she had a seat across from Stacey.

Shell realized she'd put the spotlight unfairly on Hannah when she didn't really want it, so she turned it to someone else. "At least you aren't bunking next door to that one," she pointed at Stacey.

Stacey sat up, a smile on her face. "Hey, I make no excuses and I offer no apologies."

Liz had a seat at the table with the rest of them, motioning for Marie to join them. "Why don't we enjoy our first cup of coffee together, and then we'll get busy."

That sounded excellent to Hannah. When she'd been little and wanted sisters, this is the exact type of situation she'd thought of, and she loved this group of women as if they were her sisters. "Anybody interested in hitting up the Black Friday sales tomorrow? As in the national shopping holiday, not our men," she clarified.

"I'm just going to say it." Liz set her coffee cup down. "Do I need to, you know, buy stuff for a possible grandchild?"

Again Hannah struggled to swallow her coffee. "Jesus Christ, mom," she mumbled.

"She opened the door, I'm stepping through it." Marie looked over at her, her gaze penetrating so much, like her son's did. "What are your plans?"

"There aren't any right now." She shrugged. "We haven't sat down and talked about it at length. We've mentioned it off-hand. I mean, I'm sure it's coming. Garrett's not getting any younger, and I do want children," she trailed off.

"But is it coming in the next year?" Marie pressured. "This is what we need to know."

"I'm not God." Her tone was sarcastic. "I can't tell you when it's going to happen."

"Hannah, don't be a smartass," Liz told her. "We're excited."

"Not to mention, he's hot, you're hot, the children that the two of you make will be out of this world," Shell offered.

A deep voice rumbled in the room. "Who's kid? Han?"

Her head dropped onto her arm. "Nothing," she told Garrett. "They're being dumb."

"Is there something you need to tell me?" he asked.

She took a deep breath and turned to face him. When she did, her mouth went bone dry. He stood in the kitchen in a pair of sweat pants, no shirt, and his hair was lying haphazardly on his head. She may have pulled it a bit too hard the night before, she decided as she got up to go stand in front of him. "We'll be right back," she told the group.

"What were they talking about? Granted, I'm fuzzy because I just woke up, but were they saying that you're pregnant?" he asked, shock in his voice.

"No." She shook her head. "I'm not, remember, I have that little IUD that makes sure I don't have any slip ups? They want me to be, but that's them. You know we haven't really sat down and talked about that yet, and you also know that I want a few months alone with you before we do. They're just excited because I have time off. I could have a child if we decide to."

"I gotta say," he blew out a breath and she smelled the mint of his toothpaste, "for a split second I was super excited, and then I was fucking terrified."

She leaned up on her tiptoes and kissed him softly, hooking her arms around his waist when he caught her around the neck and deepened the caress.

"Morning," he told her as he pulled back.

"Morning." She licked her lips and pulled her bottom one between her teeth. "Speaking of, why are you even up right now?"

"I woke up alone. Both you and Havock were gone, and I didn't want to be by myself. I figure I can watch some TV and listen to you ladies gossip and bitch, take a little cat nap, and be ready to eat when it's time."

"Sounds like a good plan," she told him, walking him over to the couch.

He lay down, and she covered him up with the blanket they'd been keeping on it. She leaned down and kissed his cheek, stopping when he caught her by the wrist. "For the record, you'd make an incredible mom."

"Thanks." She grinned. "I hope so, but when the time comes and not before. We'll know when we're ready."

"This game fucking sucks," Kevin growled, disgusted at the football game he watched on TV.

"Who knew these guys got so serious about a game," Hannah whispered. She never even knew that Garrett watched sports.

"Come the fuck on," Jared yelled. "Break the tackle, dude, you weigh three hundred pounds."

"Five yards, that's all we needed. Five goddamn yards," Robert said, surprising his daughter.

"This is embarrassing." Garrett threw the remote down.

"And really fucking boring," Stacey whispered back at the ladies.

They all giggled because they agreed.

"How much more time does the turkey need, Mom?" Hannah asked, ready to eat.

Liz walked over and opened the oven, then called Marie over. The two of them both gave their opinions and told the younger women that they thought it was ready. It made Hannah happy that her mom and Marie seemed to be getting along well. It was important for her to have them be friends. Their lives would never be normal, and that would mean that sometimes everyone would have to see each other at the same time. It wouldn't work if they didn't get along.

"Let me get the guys," Marie told them.

"God be with you, lady, for interrupting that," Shell threw out, having a seat at the table.

"Do you want some wine?" Hannah asked her. It wasn't often that they pulled out the good bottle, and none of the guys liked it, but they did every once in a while.

"Ohhh yeah, that'll be a nice change of pace." Shell's phone buzzed at her side. She hesitated to pick it up. It was the holidays and the guys were making their way into the room, but she worried that it was someone who needed her or needed an answer to a question. Glancing down, she did a double take; she wasn't sure if what she'd seen was her imagination or if it was the truth or not. "Holy fuck," she breathed.

"Could we please put the f-word away for the rest of the day?" Hannah asked, setting the glass of wine in front of Shell.

"No, you're gonna wanna say it when I tell you what this message says."

Hannah doubted that highly. "You know I don't even cuss, usually."

"Oh, you do sometimes," Garrett piped up, a shit-eating grin on his face.

Hannah cleared her throat. "Can we not just have a quiet family dinner?"

"We sure can," Shell said. "And I'd like to get a picture of you and Garrett, if I could."

Hannah went over and sat in Garrett's lap, smiling as Shell snapped a picture, asking them to pose for one more. "I'm not sure why you want one; you have to have a ton of pictures of the two of us. Why do you need another one?"

Putting her phone out in front of her face and fixing the camera, Shell shrugged. "Just wanted to get the look on your faces when y'all found out for the first time that your duet went to number one on the all-genre chart."

She said it so off-handed that it took a few seconds for the words to sink in, but when they did, the looks on their faces were priceless, and Shell had never been so excited to capture the moment on camera.

Tears were shed, hugs were given, and fists were pumped as the small group congratulated the couple.

"Did you ever think it?" Liz asked.

"No, not at all," Hannah answered, humble as ever. "I hoped, especially when I saw how many hits it was getting on YouTube. I've been getting messages about people using it at their wedding too, so I knew it was popular, but no, never in my wildest dreams did I imagine all-genre," she squealed, pulling Garrett into another hug.

"Would it be in bad taste for me to somehow get Bryson's phone number and text something along the lines of 'suck my dick' to him?" Garrett asked. He knew without a doubt that they wouldn't be hearing anything from him, hopefully ever again. There were certain people that Jared knew in dark places and they'd done some checking on Bryson—he wasn't as clean as he liked people to think.

Hannah shook her head. "Yes! You know this is killing him even more than the beating you gave him yesterday. According to what he said to you, what he wanted more than anything was the number one, and we got it, baby!"

He exhaled a breath. Everything that the two of them had been through had been working towards this moment. Their friends, their family, their dog, a number one song. He had known as soon as he'd kissed her that Hannah was going to be the person he spent the rest of his life with. To know that she was going to be there, no matter how ugly the world got, no matter how tired he was at the end of the—meant everything.

"So," Liz asked as she stood. "Who's hungry? Let's celebrate!"

Epilogue

New Year's Even

Hannah could hear the noise of the crowd as she made her way, along with the guys of Black Friday, towards the stage. New Years Eve was *the* night to have a concert, and out of sheer luck, the guys had managed to snag Nashville for the night. This would also be the opening night of their tour.

They'd all thought they'd have a few more weeks off, but when New Year's Eve had opened up, they decided to go for it. Hannah was all for it. As long as she was with Garrett, there was nowhere she wouldn't go.

"Have I told you how hot you look tonight?" he asked, putting his mouth next to her ear so that she could hear him over the noise that was just beyond the curtains.

"No." She pouted. "And I dressed up in this just for you." She smiled up at him.

His arm went around her, resting his hand on her hip, half of his palm on her ass. He gave it a tiny squeeze and she jumped. "The little black dress does it for me."

Obviously, if the look in his eyes gave any indication of how much he liked it. "I'm glad." She kissed his cheek. The heels that she wore put them closer to the same height, but he still had a head length over her.

"Heels are fucking hot too." He looked down at the hot pink stilettos she wore.

"Do I need to go change before I join you onstage for our duet?" she asked, clasping his free hand in hers.

He breathed deeply. "Nah, it'll just give me something to look forward to when we get done with the show. Then you and I can have our own little party to ring in the New Year. How's that sound?"

"Perfect." She stepped back as the guys started to circle.

"Two minutes, guys," Mike told them.

"Give me a kiss," he told her, grasping her hips to bring her back where she had been before.

She did as she was told, and then waited as they chanted something that she couldn't make out, but made her laugh anyway. "I'll see you later," she told him.

"Don't make me wait when I call you out," he warned.

Hannah didn't. When he called her out, she came out to an amazing cheer from the crowd, and they sat closely together, singing the duet that had made them both bigger stars together than they had ever been separately. As they finished, Hannah stood up and took a small bow. Grasping Garett's hand she pulled him in for a kiss. This was exactly what she'd been missing when she'd met him. She hadn't known it then, but she knew it now, and she would never give it up for anything that anyone promised her—there was no monetary value they could put on the price of love.

The End

Book #3 in the Rockin' Country Series

(Will also include an exclusive Rockin' Country Novella!!)
Coming early 2015

Prologue

Hannah looked out over the German crowd; ninety thousand strong, as Black Friday performed their set for the summer festival. She was so thankful she had taken this time off. If she hadn't, she wouldn't be here for this, and she knew that she wouldn't want to miss it. Garrett held the huge crowd in the palm of his hand. Every time he asked them to do something, they did it without hesitating. She had never seen this many people before in her life. These rock festivals were much larger than the country festivals that she attended.

"Amazing, isn't it?"

She glanced up at Shell, nodding. "It is. I can't believe all these people have been out in this intense heat all day."

From where she stood, Garrett was in the shadow of the setting sun, and his silhouette was beautiful against it.

Pulling her phone out, she snapped a few pictures, uploading one of them to her Instagram account. So far, everyone that had told her the fans would love to get glimpses into their private life was right. Any picture she uploaded of the two of them got more likes than the last one. Pictures of just him were probably the most popular, but she didn't let that affect her one way or another. Since taking her break in November, she had been careful to keep the posts at a regular interval. Call her crazy, but it was important for her to keep them informed. She didn't want to lose the fans that meant so much to her, no matter what she ended up deciding about her career. The past six months had been amazing, and she knew that she would never give them up for anything.

"Are you nervous?" Shell asked, a soft smile on her face.

"Kind of. I mean we didn't expect for this to happen so soon. We thought it would take longer," she told her friend, putting her hand on her stomach that, even though still flat, held a little bit of extra weight.

"The two of you are magnetic together, I'm pretty sure that as soon as he looked at you when you went off birth control, it was like boom, pregnant."

Hannah laughed. "Kind of." She turned her attention back to the concert, watching Garrett.

He was now the father of her child. Conceived in early April, they were expecting the birth in January. It still wasn't ideal. While she would be off, he would still be touring, but by the time she had to go back to work, the baby would be six months old and hopefully on some type of schedule.

"Stop thinking ahead. I can see the panic on your face," Shell told her. "We'll deal with it, no matter what it is."

She knew that Shell spoke the truth. Her attorney had found a clause in some of the legal language that would allow her to terminate a portion of her contract if she so wanted to. It would allow her to take off as much time as she wanted, up to two years, after the birth of a child. Hannah still wasn't sure what she wanted to do, but she figured that by the time all of that rolled around, she would know. Her CD was still selling well, the lyric videos released on social media were well over the millions of views, and the record company was happy that she was still active. Right now, they were all happy. She hoped it would continue to be that way. Just that morning, she had let the record company know she was pregnant, and they seemed okay with it. She was relieved they hadn't asked her to get an abortion; she had heard of that before, even had a few friends in the music industry that had done it at the suggestion of a record company. It would ruin their image and their career, they had been told. For her and Garrett, this was planned, a symbol of the love that they shared for one another—only they hadn't expected it so quickly. She smiled as she thought back to the morning she'd woken up feeling sick, wondering if the one time they'd tried, it had taken. He had been so freaked out when she went to take the pregnancy test, and then he'd gone white when she'd come out of the bathroom holding it, not needing the five minutes it was supposed to take.

"I can't believe I'm here right now." Hannah gestured out to the crowd and then looked back at her husband. He wore a T-shirt with the armholes cut out—white in deference to the hot day. Sweat caused the material to stick to his body. The longer hair style he now sported caused his hair to curl up at the ends, and she hoped with everything she had at that moment they had a son that looked like him. She would love for their child to have the curly hair he got once it got long enough. He looked over at her and she could feel his gaze, even though she couldn't see his eyes behind the sunglasses.

"My wife is here today," he was saying to the crowd. "I'd like to invite her out here, if it's okay with you?" There was a huge uproar from them, clapping and whistling.

They hadn't talked about this. She knew that he wanted to make the announcement today, but she hadn't been aware that he wanted her to go out and be with him.

"C'mon, babe." He crooked his finger at her.

She was immediately glad she had taken the time to put her hair in a braid. The black shorts she wore weren't too short, and the tank-top she wore was billowy enough that no one could make out the fact that she had gained a few pounds. She pushed her sunglasses over her eyes and walked out onto the stage. It was breathtaking to see that many people in one spot, and it felt like it took forever until she reached where he stood. He held his hand out to her.

"So everybody, this is my gorgeous wife, Harmony." He toyed with the braid that rested over her shoulder.

Not sure what to do, she waved out to the crowd.

"Say hi." He held the mic up to her mouth.

"Hi," she giggled, nerves getting the better of her.

The crowd was so loud she was afraid they would knock her down with their response.

"They love you almost as much as I do." He stood behind her and grabbed her around the waist.

He dropped the mic to his side and moved his mouth to her ear. "Do you wanna tell them?"

"We can if you want. Everyone who needs to know already does."

He dropped a kiss on her nose, and the crowd went wild. "The reason I brought her out here is because we wanted to share something with all of you."

Hannah held on tightly to his hand that spanned her stomach. If he hadn't been holding her up, she was afraid she would have slid down in the face of all these people. The crowd continued to yell as he waited; they grew louder and louder until he put the mic back up his mouth.

"Okay, okay. You wanna know, I'll tell you. Sometime in the New Year, there will be a little Reaper or Harmony running around. She's pregnant."

The roar of the crowd was so loud and the enthusiasm so much that they both physically took a step back. At some point a "kiss her" chant started, and Garrett smiled at her, pulling her to him. "Now that the cat's out of the bag, we don't have to worry about keeping secrets anymore."

"We sure don't." She wrapped her arms around his neck, squealing when he bent to pick her up and put her legs around his waist.

This time the picture that went around the world was the one of them lip-locked in front of ninety-thousand fans in hundred-degree weather. It would be the most popular picture of the two of them for months.

Connect with Laramie

Website:

http://www.laramiebriscoe.com

Facebook:

https://www.facebook.com/AuthorLaramieBriscoe

Twitter:

https://twitter.com/LaramieBriscoe

Pinterest:

http://www.pinterest.com/laramiebriscoe/

Instagram:

http://instagram.com/laramie_briscoe

Substance B:

http://substance-b.com/LaramieBriscoe.html

Acknowledgments

This has been the most amazing journey of my life, and I wouldn't have gotten here if it weren't for the many people that have already been listed in the front of this book.

The people that come together to make up the Indie Publishing Industry are some of the best around, and I'm one of the luckiest people ever to get to work with them.

There are too many people to name, but know that all of you that have ever spoken with me, left me a message, sent me an email (whether it be good or bad), or just supported me by liking my page on Facebook…I truly and greatly appreciate it!

Also by Laramie Briscoe

Meant To Be
Heaven Hill Series #1

Prologue

Denise Cunningham pulled back the curtains covering the window pane in her front door with shaky hands. The knock that had sounded moments before wasn't the gentle knock of a friend over for a visit. Staring back at her through the glass, she saw two Warren County Sheriff's deputies holding papers. Dread rolled up in her throat as her stomach began to churn. She let the blinds fall and took two deep breaths before she unlocked the door and faced the men standing on the other side. As she stepped out, the brightness of the sun assaulted her eyes, the warmth of the summer day made it even more difficult to breathe past the lump in her throat.

"Denise Cunningham?" The taller of the two asked.

Not trusting her voice, she could only nod her head in acknowledgement of who she was.

With cold efficiency, he handed her the papers in his hands. "Denise Cunningham, I'm serving you with papers from Kentucky Housing." He produced a pen and requested her signature.

In minutes it was over. The scene she had dreaded most over the last few months had come to fruition. Unless she could come up with six months back mortgage, she would lose her home. She stood frozen in shock as the officers walked away from the door and headed back to their patrol car. It almost made her laugh – the fact that they felt she, a single mother, was dangerous enough to warrant two deputies. As they pulled away, she realized her neighbors watched. Shame and embarrassment caused her face to burn as she slammed her door shut.

Tears came now, along with shakes that wracked her body. "God, please help me," she whispered as she opened the packet of paperwork they had left with her. "What am I going to do?" Through the tears, she read the legal papers in her trembling hands. The amount due was more than she had seen in years. Especially now that her hours had recently been cut. She was officially screwed.

The shrill ringing of her cell phone broke into her freakout. A number she had never seen before displayed on the screen, and she wondered if she should answer it. Along with the money she owed on her home, she owed thousands to credit card companies. They had also begun to hound her. Should she take the chance and answer it or let the voicemail pick it up? As she debated, her finger hit the *accept* button of its own accord.

"Hello?"

"Denise, this is Roni," the voice on the other end greeted.

Roni was in fact Sharon Walker, another employee at

the big box store where Denise had found a temporary job. They'd only spoken a time or two, and Denise hadn't actually been sure the other woman would ever call her. To say this was a surprise was an understatement. But at this point, anything that took her mind off of what had just happened was welcome.

"Hey, Roni."

"Did I catch you at a bad time? It took you a while to answer. I'm gonna ask you for a favor, so if you can't do it, just let me know," she forged ahead in a rush.

A bad time? Was it couth to tell a mere acquaintance that your home was about to be foreclosed on?

Clearing her throat Denise said, "Not at all. What can I help you with?" Accepting a favor for someone would possibly get her out of the house, the house that soon would no longer be hers. The walls were closing in, and she needed something to do. She needed something to work out halfway good for once instead of all the gloom and doom.

"Can you cover my shift for me tonight? I've got a little bit of an emergency with my brother, and I'm gonna need a few hours."

Denise bit her lip. She had heard rumblings about Roni's brother. Word around town had it that he was part of a major outlaw biker gang called the Heaven Hill Motorcycle Club. Whatever Roni would be doing to help her brother would probably be illegal. Would that make Denise an accomplice?

"Would it make you a what?" Roni asked as Denise stood frozen with the phone to her ear.

Shit. She'd said that out loud. "Nevermind. I'll cover for you. What time do I have to be there?" Anything would be better than sitting here, worrying about things she had no control over.

Roni rattled off a time that would only allow her minutes to get dressed, head out the door, and make it there just in time to clock in. Quickly they hung up. Depression threatening to take over, Denise shoved the packet of paperwork under the pillow of her couch. With any luck neither of her children would see it. Their lives had been in as much upheaval as hers. They didn't need to see this too – she felt like a failure as their mother.

Pulling out of her Plum Springs subdivision, Denise made her way to Louisville road which took her to the interstate. The interstate would take her less time than going through town. She made sure to take in her surroundings. Unless a miracle happened or she hit the lottery, her days living in this neighborhood were numbered. A red light stopped her right before she hit the interstate. To the left, blue lights could be seen swirling on top of police cars. Men were being hand-cuffed and put in back seats two at a time. It wasn't unusual to see arrests right next to the interstate, but this time she noticed an influx of motorcycles. The gas station on Duntov Way, situated between a fast food restaurant and a liquor store, usually didn't see a lot of motorcycles. The exception being Harley Weekend at the local dragstrip. With keen eyes, she got a good look at the patches that adorned the backs of the leather vests, or cuts as they called them, the men wore.

"Fuck," she breathed, recognizing the patch on most of the men. The Heaven Hill insignia inside a skull. The bottom rocker on the cut indicated this was the Bowling Green Chapter.

It was the Heaven Hill Motorcycle Club, and, if she wasn't mistaken, she had just seen Roni's brother get put in the back of a sheriff's patrol car. Probably by the same officers that had just served her. If there was one thing she knew, it was that all hell was about to break loose in small-town Kentucky.

Made in the USA
Monee, IL
22 September 2022

14476284R00152